I0731894

MY BEST GAMBLE

Brianna's Story

CAROLE WOLFE

Blind Vista Press

Copyright © 2022 Carole Wolfe

All rights reserved.

www.carolewolfe.com

First Edition

ISBN 978-1-7371985-3-6 (EPUB edition)
ISBN 978-1-7371985-4-3 (Paperback edition)
ISBN 978-1-7371985-5-0 (Large print paperback edition)

This is a work of fiction. Names, characters, businesses, places, events, locales, and incidents are either the products of the author's imagination or used in a fictitious manner. Any resemblance to actual persons, living or dead, or actual events is purely coincidental.

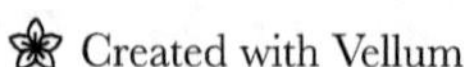 Created with Vellum

Chapter 1

Brianna trudged up the stairs to her apartment. All she wanted to do was kick off her four-inch stilettos and wiggle out of her skin-tight leather pants. Her toes ached with each step.

At least her brain was numb. It had fallen asleep ten minutes into her date with Richie. He'd rated a solid nine on her possible boyfriend rating system, but dinner proved he was a two—maybe three—at best. The entire meal, he couldn't stop talking about how he was the best tattoo artist in the city. Brianna hadn't lived in Las Vegas long, but she suspected Richie wasn't even in the top ten. She'd watched enough *Ink Masters* on Netflix to know this guy was clueless.

Not only that, but Richie "forgot" his wallet, leaving her stuck with the bill for the high-end steak restaurant he'd insisted they try. There would be no second date . . . unless, of course, she checked to make sure he had his wallet before they left.

She reached the third-floor hallway and made her way to apartment 3B. Noise from the television drifted into the hallway. It was a telltale sign her roommate was vegging out on the couch.

Brianna leaned against the doorframe as she dug in her purse for the key to the apartment. Her hand passed over her bottle of pepper spray, an extra-large container of hand sanitizer, and her flip phone before her fingers connected with the warm fuzziness of the rabbit's foot that decorated her house key.

Shoving the key into the lock, Brianna shook and rattled the door handle as she began the adventure of entering her apartment. The landlord had promised to take care of it, but ever since his son's girlfriend's ex-uncle-in-law checked it out, the lock took skill, determination, and a little finesse to operate.

A sharp pain shot up from Brianna's toes. Naomi hated to be interrupted while she binge-watched reality TV, but if Brianna didn't get off her feet quick, she'd never be able to fit into her pumps for work the next morning.

She rapped on the door with what she hoped was a polite request and waited. The volume of the television got louder. Apparently, a show about horrible dermatologic conditions was more important than answering the door.

Brianna knocked again while continuing to work the doorknob.

"No solicitors," came the reply, and Brianna shook her head.

"It's me. The lock isn't working. Open the door."

"Who's me?"

Brianna rested her forehead on the door while she answered. "Brianna. Your roommate."

The volume of the television reduced slightly, and Brianna heard footsteps. Letting out a sigh of relief, she tossed her key back into her purse and waited. The door squeaked open as far as the security chain would allow, and Naomi's eye peeked out.

"You have a key. Why don't you use it?"

Brianna shifted her weight as pain shot through her heel. "The lock's jammed. Didn't you hear me try?"

The door shut, and for a moment Brianna thought she would be left to sleep in the hallway. Before she could put down her purse, though, the door swung open, and she saw Naomi's retreating form as her roommate returned to her perch on the couch.

"Did you go by the grocery store on your way home? We're out of rocky road ice cream." Naomi wrapped herself in the afghan Brianna's mom had sent her for Christmas. It had arrived beautiful and perfect, but Naomi had stained it with red wine and Cheetos. At least Brianna's parents lived far away and couldn't see how disrespectful her roommate was.

Sliding off her shoes, Brianna sank to the floor and rubbed her toes. "No. After the date from hell ended, I came straight home."

Naomi's eyes didn't leave the screen. She watched attentively as the dermatologist forced a creamy yellowish substance out of an incision on the patient's head. Brianna turned away, the filet mignon and mushrooms sauteed in béarnaise sauce she'd paid for earlier threatening to reappear. Concentrating on her feet, she continued massaging her toes until the tingling stopped.

"If it was that bad, then you need ice cream, too." Naomi snagged the quart of ice cream from its perch on the side table and hugged it close to her. "This one's mine."

Rather than argue, Brianna stood up and picked up her shoes and purse. "I'm going to bed. I have to be at work early tomorrow."

"That's why you had a crappy date. You probably screwed it up yourself so you could come home early. All you ever do is work. If you want to find a proper boyfriend, you need to put as much effort into it as you do that stupid job of yours."

The television volume increased, signaling the conversation was over. Knowing the drill, Brianna headed to her bedroom. She closed the door behind her and went straight to her closet. She tossed her purse and shoes inside.

Next, she peeled off the leather pants, draping them over the padded hanger and tucking them into the far end of her closet. She pulled off her T-shirt and threw it into the hamper. As soon as the soft jersey pajama top hit her skin, Brianna relaxed for the first time all evening.

Grabbing her tote of toiletries, she eased the door open and tiptoed down the hallway to the bathroom. Naomi blared the volume of the television however loud she wanted, but Brianna had learned quickly that her roommate didn't appreciate any noise during her shows. Sometimes Brianna waited in her room for a commercial, but after tonight's disaster date, she wanted to wash away any evidence she'd bothered to dress up for such a creep.

Her luck held, and she made it to the bathroom without incident. Her fake lashes came off first, and she placed them back into their storage container. Makeup wipes took off most of the foundation and what was left of her lipstick. She smiled when she turned on the hot tap and was rewarded with warmish water to cleanse her face. The landlord had promised to fix the hot water heater soon, but Brianna didn't hold out hope. She patted on nighttime moisturizer and eye cream before brushing out her long brunette hair. Not for the first time, Brianna wished she could afford to highlight her hair again. She was a better blonde than a brunette, and she had proof that blondes did have more fun.

"But they get into more trouble as well," she murmured to herself as she put her toiletries back in her tote and crept to her room. Brianna paused to listen to the commercial advertising a psychic.

"Dead-end job? Horrible dating record? Roommate got you down? I can help. Laney Lifeline here. If you need some direction for your life, I'm your answer. Palm reading, tarot cards, looking into your soul. I can do it all. If you want to course-correct your life, give me a call."

Brianna shook her head as she closed the door. She didn't need a psychic to know what caused her problems—or, more specifically, who. She'd been happy selling real estate in Saint Thomas. Top sales associate for three years running. It was easy to sell people houses when you were surrounded by tropical beaches and beautiful weather.

Brianna sighed. She would still be enjoying the sun and surf if she hadn't mixed business with pleasure. She'd been warned about falling for clients, but Brianna ignored the advice. And look what it cost her: her job, her home, her savings.

The thought of what Doug Gerome had taken from her brought tears to her eyes. He'd appeared in her office one afternoon looking for a vacation home. She'd found him the ideal place and, along the way, decided he was the man of her dreams.

"My nightmares is more like it," she mumbled as she brushed away the tears. After all was said and done, Brianna had left paradise humiliated. She had chased Doug and her money until her friend, Shelby, convinced her to come to Las Vegas. If only she'd accepted the offer to stay in Shelby's guest room. Then she wouldn't be living in a dilapidated apartment, working a thankless job to make ends meet while trying to get a real estate license in Nevada.

Tucking the tote back where it belonged, Brianna pulled back the covers of her bed and crawled in. She rolled to her side, thinking about the psychic commercial. If it was that easy to fix one's life, then everyone would be doing it.

Chapter 2

"Good morning. Dunderblatt and Watson. How may I direct your call?"

Not for the first time, Brianna wondered why Alex Dunderblatt and John Watson, partners in real estate—and sometimes crime, as she'd observed from the books she balanced—thought it would be a good idea to name their firm after themselves. The name Dunderblatt didn't inspire confidence of any kind. In fact, on more than one occasion, it made clients laugh. And not in a good way.

Poor John Watson. She had no way of knowing if his parents were huge fans of Doyle's mystery series or if they had unintentionally inflicted the sidekick's name on their son. Either way, it seemed like unnecessary punishment.

To top it off, there was no one else in the office to direct any calls to. Brianna was their one and only employee.

The grating voice that responded sent shivers down Brianna's spine. It reminded her of first grade when the class clown scraped his fingernails down the chalkboard to get a laugh. The sound didn't amuse her, now *or* then.

"I'm interested in the listing you have for the house on 658

Broken Arrow Avenue. It says Mr. Dunderblatt is the listing agent. Is he available?"

Brianna remembered Alex's condition when he had stumbled into the office earlier this morning, wearing the same clothes as the day before. An icepack hid part of a black eye, but it didn't disguise his rumpled hair or the bloodshot exposed eye. He'd grunted, which Brianna interpreted as code for, "No interruptions while I sleep off this hangover," before locking himself in his office. That was three hours ago.

"I'm sorry. He's in with a client right now. I'd be happy to help you."

She spent the next fifteen minutes talking up the fixer-upper that Alex had gotten from the bank's foreclosure department. If his friend weren't a loan officer there and able to give him first dibs on distressed properties, Brianna didn't know how Alex would have any business. As it was, she had sold the last few houses herself, even though she still didn't have her real estate license yet.

When she had taken the receptionist job two months ago, part of her employment package included time to complete the prelicensing requirements as well as payment of her exam and license fees. She hadn't made much progress on the exam or license, since she spent most of her time answering phones and covering for Alex when he was hungover. She considered going to John about the situation, but she'd never actually met him. She suspected he was an imaginary person based the unoccupied status of his office.

"It sounds perfect for what we need," the client said. "When can we see it?"

Brianna pulled up Alex's calendar on her computer and grimaced when she noticed he'd blocked off the entire day. Tequila hangovers were the worst. She'd never mess with Alex again when he was recovering from one of those.

Despite the fact she had no license, she had no other choice but to show the property herself. She calculated how much time it would take her to get from the showing back to her apartment in order to be ready for her date at five. She'd shrugged off Richie's bad manners from the previous night and moved on to Lenny. They were catching the early-bird special at her favorite restaurant. Even if the date was a disaster, Brianna knew the salmon and roasted fingerling potatoes would be worth the trip.

"I could meet you this afternoon at two thirty. Does that work for you?"

She shouldn't be scheduling appointments for herself, but there was no other way around it. Between her perpetually drunk employer and her mysteriously missing one, she was the only person who made any money for this firm.

"Let's make it three thirty. See you then."

Before she could protest, the client hung up. She put down the phone and realized she didn't have his name or number to call him back. "Safety first" used to be her mantra. When she sold real estate in Saint Thomas, she ran background checks on occasion. It had worked until Doug. Now all bets were off.

She shook her head. Brianna promised herself she wouldn't waste any more time thinking about Doug. He'd stolen enough from her as it was. There was no way she was letting him steal her new start as well.

The rest of the day passed as usual, although she did manage to complete two review modules for the real estate license test between answering the phone, returning emails, and getting Alex's lunch. His hangover remedy for days like this included a bag of tacos, queso, and chips, which she left outside his office door with a small bottle of ibuprofen.

Afterwards, she took a picture of the sticky note she left him, *Running some firm errands. Phone forwarded to answering service. Be back tomorrow at 8. B.,* and saved it with all the other documentation she kept in case someone asked about her whereabouts. Alex never acknowledged her notes, and she doubted he read them, but she kept leaving them anyway.

She scooped up her purse, full of brochures about the property she was showing as well as a few other dumps she thought might be of interest to this client, and headed out the door. If all went well, by the time she got to her date, another property from Dunderblatt and Watson would be sold.

▭

RUSHING INTO THE RESTAURANT, Brianna checked the time: five thirty. She took a few quick breaths to steady herself. The afternoon had proven to be more of a challenge than she'd expected.

She'd spent her time avoiding her client's grabby hands and ignoring numerous rude, crude, and completely inappropriate suggestions about how she could help him make a decision. Brianna had convinced him to buy the property while assuring him he didn't have a chance in hell with her. All she needed to do now was draw up the contract for Alex's approval in the morning.

But the professional victory had made her late for her date. Not that it really mattered. She had a feeling she'd wind up paying for this dinner, too, if she wanted anything other than water and complimentary bread.

She stopped inside the door and pulled her compact from her purse. A quick glance in the mirror told her she needed to visit the ladies' room before she sat down, but the hostess appeared.

"Do you have a reservation?"

"Yes. I'm meeting someone, but I'm late and I need to detour to the restroom to fix myself up. Reservation was under Brown. It was for five."

The hostess checked her monitor. "The Brown party checked in. They're working on their entrées right now."

"Is there another Brown party? It's a pretty common

name." She gave a forced laugh. "I doubt my date would start without me."

The hostess's eyes widened, and Brianna recognized pity in them.

"Oh. You're the blind date." She reached under her station and pulled out a napkin. Her perfectly manicured fingers dangled it by the corner, touching it as little as possible, like it had cooties. "This is for you."

Brianna took the note. Ignoring a sense of dread, she unfolded it. She wasn't surprised as she read it.

Didn't think you were coming. Found someone else. Good luck.

More embarrassed that the hostess had read the note than by her blind date ditching her, Brianna comforted herself: This guy wasn't the one. The "one" was out there somewhere.

Brianna looked the hostess in the eye and asked, "Is a table available? I need to eat."

The hostess clicked her tongue. "Sorry. We're full tonight."

Brianna pointed to a vacant seat at the bar between two men. "What about there?"

"That seat's reserved." Her eyes shifted to something behind Brianna, and she said, "Can you step aside? I have guests waiting."

Brianna moved out of the way, confused by the hostess's curt reaction. She considered her next move when an earthy-smelling cologne tickled her nose. Glancing up, she noticed a man dressed in leather from head to toe urging the diamond-draped woman on his arm closer to the hostess.

The woman's nose wrinkled up as they passed. "Some people need to understand they don't belong."

Brianna's cheeks heated with embarrassment, and she turned to leave. It was bad enough she got stood up, but for someone else to be rude for no reason made her feel worse. The only thing she wanted to do now was grab takeout and retreat to her apartment. It meant another night avoiding

Naomi, but that option was better than standing here in a restaurant letting strangers judge her.

Brianna hurried out the door, stopping to hold it open for a couple. The man let his date pass through first before nodding at Brianna. She smiled back, but the smile died on her face when the man's date grabbed his arm and yanked him forward.

"What is it with everyone tonight?" she muttered to herself as she left the restaurant behind. Brianna took off down the street, looking for something to replace the salmon and potatoes she wouldn't be getting after all.

She passed a burger joint, then a pizza place before her stomach responded to the sight of the Greek food truck sitting in front of the park. A gyro would hit the spot. And if she was lucky, she might even snag some baklava. Finally, her night was looking up!

Chapter 3

After a short wait and a debate with the food truck vendor about the gyro meat's origin story, Brianna took her food into the park. People-watching was one of her favorite pastimes. She'd planned to indulge herself at the restaurant, but since that fell through, she might as well make the most of her evening.

Brianna found a bench and unpacked her dinner. The taste of the soft pita bread filled with fresh lamb, tomatoes, onions, cucumbers, and creamy tzatziki sauce kept her busy for a few minutes. She'd skipped the french fries, only because the food truck was serving *galaktoboureko* instead of baklava. The thick custard slice waited in a clamshell takeout container for her to devour. It would be a reward for her long day. She couldn't wait to indulge.

Energy pulsed around her. A few families came out to play after dinner, but it was the gatherings of adults that drew her attention. Couples on dates wandered along paved pathways, holding hands and whispering in each other's ears. Wisps of jealousy teased her, but she ignored them.

It's not their fault my date didn't work out.

A group of women walked by her, talking loudly enough that she could hear their conversation.

"You shouldn't use those store-brand laundry detergents." A woman wearing various shades of beige leaned closer to her friend as she continued. "They're full of chemicals and harmful ingredients. I told you how Amanda broke out in hives because of the perfumes."

Her friend, who stood out in her hot-pink tank top and white jeans, shook her head. "Lindsey, you think everything is bad for us. If I followed your advice, I would use nothing but water and vinegar."

The beige lady shook her head. "You can clean almost anything with those two things, and they're safe for the environment and for your family. Don't you want to preserve Earth for future generations?"

A third woman, this one wearing a polka-dot wrap dress, frowned. "You sound like my son's teacher. Always complaining that things aren't good enough. Why would companies make things if they're going to harm people?"

The group moved on, leaving Brianna to ponder the question on her own. Her immediate answer was that money made the world go 'round. Those big companies added perfumes and dyes and chemicals and whatever else because it generated money.

Which was something she needed, too.

Leaning back on the hard bench, she calculated how much money she would need to leave Naomi behind and live on her own again. At one time, she'd been financially independent and enjoyed a life without roommates.

That was before Doug had entered her life. If it weren't for him, she wouldn't be indulging in a high-calorie dessert on her own. She'd be sharing it with a man.

"It isn't my fault."

The child's voice pulled her out of her thoughts, and she looked up to see a boy arguing with his sister. They reminded her of Blake and Libby, Doug's children. She'd met them a few times and sent them gifts and cards. The familiar feeling of guilt popped up as she recalled the fight she'd had with Doug the last time she was around the kids. Embarrassment at her behavior made her face feel hot, and she looked down so no one could see her reddened cheeks.

She remembered what her mother had told her the last time they talked.

"Your ability to judge people's character is lacking, Brianna. It would help if you wouldn't surround yourself with men who take advantage of you."

"But how am I supposed to know what a guy is like if I don't make an effort to get to know him?"

Her mother had sighed, something she did a lot when they talked about her questionable love life.

"You don't have to move in with someone to get to know him. Slow down. Take your time. Respect yourself and people will respect you."

Brianna's mother had told her that at least once a week for the last ten years, but it hadn't worked. She was still picking the wrong men to date, the wrong company to work for, and the wrong roommate to live with.

"Let's go to a casino." A man's voice interrupted Brianna's rumination. She peeked up in time to see a group of young men walking by. "I've got a feeling tonight's my lucky night."

Returning her gaze to the ground, Brianna studied the cigarette butts and business cards on the sidewalk as she listened to the men compare casinos. She'd avoided gambling since moving to Las Vegas. Not that she had a problem with gambling. It was the lack of money that created more of an issue.

Brianna opened the container holding her *galaktaboureko*. The rich dessert distracted her. The calories she didn't need, but she sighed as the creamy custard dissolved on her tongue.

She enjoyed each bite and closed her eyes to enjoy the sugar rush.

Dessert was the one thing that never let her down.

Gathering her trash, she decided she would go to a casino and reward herself with something fun. She'd stick with penny slots, which was a better plan than returning to the apartment and listening to Naomi's television show.

Brianna hopped up with excitement. She could surprise Shelby at the Diamond Casino and Hotel, where her friend worked. Brianna hadn't spent as much time with Shelby as she wanted, but maybe tonight they could catch up.

Plus, she hadn't done anything for herself in a while, and even this small decision felt good. Just because nothing else in her life worked out didn't mean she didn't deserve a little rest and relaxation. With a smile on her face, she headed toward the Diamond.

Chapter 4

It was a quick walk to the casino, even in heels. Brianna paused and admired the building. Tall ivory pillars flanked the glittering entrance doors. The turquoise lights flashed the casino's name, the color reminding Brianna of the ocean water of Saint Thomas.

Brianna pulled open the door to the casino and paused a few steps inside. Entering a casino always transported her to a new place, and she let herself take it all in. A hazy smoke filled the room, which rang with laughter and bells. Moans of defeat and loss almost covered up the joy of winning, but as usual, somehow the casino made the good bigger than the bad.

As far as she was concerned, it was all a game of chance, but it was still fun. She bought twenty dollars' worth of slot machine tokens and wandered around the floor.

Brianna kept her eyes peeled for Shelby while she looked for a slot machine to play. The search for the perfect spot was part of the adventure as far as she was concerned. Dropping a token into the machine was fun, but Brianna embraced the entire experience.

She headed to the back of the giant room, past the poker

tables and roulette wheels. The high-stakes lounge was off to the right, still cordoned off by a thick red-velvet rope. She didn't know if that meant it was too early for the people with deep pockets to show up for a game or if the rope was a subtle reminder that money did make a difference.

Rolling her eyes, she willed herself not to get sucked into the have/have not argument and focused on finding a slot machine that caught her fancy. She steered clear of the ones that were branded with popular television shows and comics. Maybe she was old-school, but she preferred the more subdued brands. What she really wanted was a true vintage slot machine, but she knew that would never happen. Casinos rarely kept them around because they were too easy to manipulate.

A row of empty machines caught her attention. The flashing blue-and-red lights announced she could win if she played. No one else was around. She made a beeline to the spot, choosing the seat in the middle. She sat down and prepared to insert a token when she felt a tap on her shoulder. Looking up, she smiled at Shelby.

"This is a nice surprise!" her friend said.

Brianna leaned forward, gave her a quick hug, then settled back in her chair.

"I wondered when you'd come visit."

"Hey there. Spur of the moment decision." Brianna took in her friend's uniform. The white button-down shirt was form-fitting, accentuating Shelby's cleavage, but not too revealing. The black leather of the pants was a perfect backdrop for the silver diamond silhouettes that decorated them. A white bowtie sported black diamond silhouettes to round things out. "You look classy. Much better than your old getup."

Brianna loved teasing her friend about the tiger costume she wore when they both worked for a pizza parlor.

Shelby put down a napkin beside the slot machine. "That

was a great job, even if the uniform was sweltering. Vodka tonic?"

Brianna debated. She really shouldn't. Her alarm was set for five thirty the next morning, but one vodka wouldn't hurt. Except if Alex came in hungover, which he would. Better to err on the side of caution.

"Soda water with a lime. Thank you."

"You know I can get you a double shot, right?"

Brianna nodded. "I have a lot to do in the morning. Need to be sharp."

Shelby shrugged as she walked off. Brianna knew Shelby didn't take it personally, but she also knew the casino liked their clients a little tipsy. Hopefully, no one would hold it against Shelby that her friend didn't want to drink.

Feeding the slot machine, Brianna took a deep breath and relaxed. Gambling wasn't something she did often, but when she did it, she immersed herself. She told herself it didn't matter if she won or lost, but she knew that was a lie.

It was like the story she told herself that it was okay to be single, without a man in her life. Intellectually, she knew being single was the best thing for her right now. She needed to focus on her job and to pass the real estate license exam. But that left her incomplete. She was accustomed to having a boyfriend. Even if it was the wrong person, it was better than being alone. Or so she thought.

Taking a deep breath, she focused on the task in front of her: the slot machine. It might not find her a man, but she might make some extra money.

In no time, Brianna tripled her money. She pulled out twenty dollars of tokens and put them in her purse. That was the best way to gamble. She could lose the rest of the money and still feel good about herself.

"I haven't seen you do that for a while," Shelby said as she set down Brianna's drink. "Your discipline's improving."

"I'm taking that as a compliment." Brianna took a sip of

her drink and grinned at the extra lime. Her friend always took care of her. "Things busy tonight?"

Nodding, Shelby said, "Crazy. Makes for great tips, but I won't be able to chat much." She glanced around the room. "You know, I'm only allowed to serve you every fifteen minutes—even though you're not really drinking—but wave me down if you need anything else. Floor manager is focused on his girlfriend tonight. Gives me more leeway."

Brianna was disappointed Shelby didn't have more time, but she understood. "Thanks. I'm pouting after getting stood up tonight. Distracting myself from the fact that nothing seems to be going my way."

That comment earned her a laugh.

"We've been over this. Nothing comes for free, and fairy tales aren't real. They're good for a bedtime story, but that's about it. You're more likely to win a million dollars playing penny slots than have the perfect life drop into your lap."

As Shelby said the words, the slot machine Brianna was playing erupted with a cacophony of bells, alarms, and flashing lights. Brianna watched in awe as tokens spewed out. When they overflowed the coin tray, Shelby handed Brianna her empty drink tray. Brianna caught the tokens and laughed.

"I don't know. Stranger things have happened. See exhibit A." She waved at the machine. "I haven't hit it this big in I-don't-know-how-long."

"Well done. For once, I'm glad to be wrong!" Shelby gave Brianna's arm a squeeze. "I've got to find another tray and get back to work. Nice to see you tonight. Don't be a stranger."

Shelby walked away, disappearing into the crowd of people swarming to the flashing lights of the slot machine. The empty seats around Brianna filled, and she was no longer secluded.

With a sigh, she gathered her winnings. It didn't make any sense to test her luck anymore. The win didn't fill the void in her savings account, but it was a step in the right direction.

Before she could head to the cashier, though, Brianna heard a scuffle and turned to see what was happening.

A woman wearing a T-shirt proclaiming "Grandmas Do It" swung her purse like a weapon to defend a slot machine from another woman resembling Olivia Newton-John's character in *Grease*. The purse connected with the spandex-clad woman's head, sending the blonde wig flying into the crowd and its owner screaming for her hair.

Stifling a laugh, Brianna stepped out of the way as security and other casino-goers rushed toward the scene. She made her way to the cashier, oblivious to the man standing in the middle of the casino floor staring at her.

Chapter 5

Doug's feet froze. He'd been searching Vegas casinos for the last few weeks in hopes of finding his ex-girlfriend. He never expected to see her win a huge jackpot right in front of him, much less walk by and not recognize him.

The blow to his ego stung. It didn't help matters that the last time he saw her she'd punched him in the face so hard he'd ended up on the floor, an embarrassing situation made worse by the fact that his ex-sister-in-law and ex-employer had witnessed it. Rubbing his chin at the memory, Doug scanned the crowd in the casino, trying to find her again when someone called out, "Get out of the way!"

Two hands rammed into Doug's shoulder, thrusting him forward. He stumbled and cursed under his breath. He looked around to see who had hit him. Several security guards rushed past. They made a beeline toward the two old ladies fighting in the corner.

He steadied himself and frowned at the commotion. Normally, he would stick around to watch the antics. But he had more important things to do right now: find his ex-girlfriend, China, and help himself to some of her winnings.

He'd seen her walk away from the slot machines, which

meant there was a good chance she was going to the cash out. He rolled his eyes. Doug gambled everything he ever won. There were no guarantees he'd get that chance again. But not China. She believed in saving for a rainy day.

Doug sauntered toward the cashier's booth as he remembered how helpful her rainy-day account had been in the past. The $100,000 he borrowed from her in Saint Thomas had funded his last business venture. Too bad it had gone south. But now that he'd found her again, he wouldn't have to take the stupid gig stealing furniture his friend had lined up for him.

He spotted her standing in line to cash out and dropped back into the shadows to watch. He sidled up to a high-top table with a half-full glass of some dark liquor on it. Grabbing it as a prop, he pretended he was enjoying a drink while he watched.

Doug's heart rate picked up when he noticed the men in line staring at his ex-girlfriend. The expressions on their faces ranged from desire and lust to hunger. While Doug felt the same way about her, anger sparked when he witnessed it in others.

A movement caught his attention. The man in line behind China reached out his hand as if he were going to grope her butt. Doug slammed down the drink and rushed toward them. Before he could get close enough, though, the line moved. China stepped forward and the man's hand whiffed through the air. Doug let out a sigh of relief and returned to his table.

"That was nice of you."

Doug looked up. He recognized the server. She'd been talking to China when she hit it big on the slot machine. Doug couldn't resist. He gave her a sly smile. This was the perfect situation for gathering information. He shoved his hands into his pockets and moved back to the table.

"Thanks."

She nodded at the glass on the table. "That looks watered down." She leaned forward to pick up the drink.

Doug took the opportunity to admire her boobs as they peeked out of the white button-down shirt and the black leather pants that fit her body like a glove.

"Can I get you another one?" she asked.

He'd already had three, but what the hell?

"Sure. Scotch, please." As she turned to leave, he put his hand on her arm. "Can I ask you something?"

The woman, whose nametag read *Shelby*, frowned. "Only if you remove your hand, please."

He released her and shook his head. Keeping his eyes averted, he chastised himself for touching the server. From experience, he had learned he got more information from women if he pretended to be shy. He needed more information on China, and Shelby might be useful.

Doug cleared his throat before he said, "Sorry. I'm trying to work up the nerve to talk to the girl who won the slots. Do you know if I have a chance?"

Shelby's eyes turned into slits. "What makes you think I know her?"

He shrugged. "You handed her the tray she's using." He pointed over his shoulder. "Her win started the commotion down by the slot machines. Hard to miss it, especially since those two women are still going at it."

Shelby studied him, as if she were thinking about what he said. Doug kept his face as pathetic-looking as possible while he waited. She tilted her head.

"Either you're really good at this or really naïve. Which is it?"

Doug knew he was close to getting the information he wanted. He gave her his best puppy dog look. "Why would you say that?"

The twinkle in her eyes told him she was going to help.

"Brianna's highly selective to say the least. I don't know if you're her type or not. But you thought to intervene with that guy in line. You've got that going for you."

Doug disguised his surprise. China had changed her name. He hadn't expected that.

"Any advice on how to approach her?"

"No." Something caught Shelby's attention, and she straightened up. "I've got to get back to work. Be right back with your drink."

Before he could stop her, she darted away. He leaned his elbows on the table and rested his chin on his hands. He had a name but not much else to go on. That was better than nothing.

He glanced back to the line at the cashier, checking on China. Doug's back tensed. The guy who had tried to grab her butt was standing at the cashier's window, but China was gone. In the time he'd been pumping Shelby for information, China had completed her transaction and left.

Fuming at his mistake, he pushed away from the table and headed toward the exit. Maybe he could catch up with her. Doug rushed to the exit and burst through the door. The dry heat hit him immediately, and he took a deep breath, filling his lungs with smoke-free air. He looked down the sidewalk both ways, but he didn't see China—no, Brianna—anywhere.

"Dammit," he mumbled before turning back to the casino. He should have known better than to talk to Shelby. Without bothering to go back inside, Doug turned in the direction of his hotel, muttering to himself, "Eyes on the prize, man. Eyes on the prize."

Chapter 6

The next day at work didn't seem as bad as usual to Brianna, but she couldn't pinpoint why. Naomi's pleasant behavior when she got home the night before could have helped. Or it might have been the security of knowing her slot machine winnings were tucked under her mattress. Or it could have been the fact that Alex came into the office on time for once—with two cups of coffee.

"Thanks for handling yesterday. I hear we have another sale." He placed a cup on her desk and perched on the edge. "Did you get full asking price for it?"

"I did." *Which you'd know if you read the paperwork I sent to you.* "All you need to do is sign the contract and I'll coordinate with Mr. Eply on the inspection and other details."

Alex's hand stopped midway to his mouth. "That property will never pass inspection. You should know better."

Resisting the urge to roll her eyes, Brianna said, "The buyer has the right to an inspection. If they want to waive it, they can. I don't think he's going to ask for one, but I have to offer it. If I don't, he'll know something is wrong."

"Has the idiot seen it?"

"Of course he has. Granted, he was busy flirting. He

might have missed a few things. Like the fact that the previous owner poured cement down the kitchen sink. Or the HVAC unit was the first one installed in the state. And the landscaping is dead and needs replacing. I positioned it as a fixer-upper. Most likely a teardown."

Her boss nodded and took a sip of his coffee. "Good thinking on your part. Distract him so he doesn't know what a piece of crap he's buying."

Without bothering to dignify the comment, Brianna looked down at her notes for the day. "You've got some calls to return. A showing later this afternoon. This one is on the repossession on Hayes Boulevard." She watched Alex's face to see if he was paying attention and shook her head when she noticed his eyes on her chest. Before she dwelled too long on the situation, she asked, "Is there anything else you need me to do today? I thought I'd leave a little early since I worked overtime yesterday."

That got Alex's attention. "Of course. You've earned it."

Brianna knew Alex hated paying time-and-a-half. If she bothered to go to a lawyer, she could probably get a sexual harassment settlement in addition to all the back pay he owed her. But she needed a job and, as she'd discovered from the client the day before, there were worse people to work for. She knew what to expect from Alex. At some point, she'd find better working conditions, but now was not the time.

"I'll finish up and head out around three." The phone rang, and she smiled at Alex. "Or would you like me to leave now and *you* answer the phone?"

Alex stood up. "Nah. Go earn your paycheck."

Brianna shook her head as he walked to his office. Guys like him only stayed afloat because girls like her took care of them. Considering she was a horrible judge of character in men, she made a note that her next boss needed to be a woman. Putting up with a woman would have to be better than this.

She answered the phone, hoping for a couple easy hours of work.

"Hi, Brianna. Brian Eply here. Let's talk about this property."

As predicted, Mr. Eply waived the inspection. He planned to gut the house and rebuild from the studs up.

"That part of town is going to be hot once enough of the area gets renovated. The early birds will definitely get the cash."

"You'll need a real estate agent to help you sell after the renovation. Give us a call. Mr. Dunderblatt would be happy to work with you again. He might give you a discount on the commission fees if you plan to flip a lot of houses." Alex would protest, but she knew lower fees would interest Eply. And if Eply was right, and the area got hot, she didn't want to miss out. "Are there any other properties you'd like to see now? I can arrange whatever showings you want."

"Email me a list of houses within a five-mile radius of this one. But you should be more focused on closing this thing. The faster the better."

"Got it. I'll let you know what I find."

Brianna sent the contract to the seller's agent. After spending an hour convincing the agent her client really didn't want to do an inspection, she still managed to squeeze in a review module for her real estate test as well as research houses for Eply, make dinner reservations for Alex and his latest fling, and catch up with filing before she left the office.

On her walk home, she stopped at the corner market. Naomi wouldn't be home until later, leaving Brianna to indulge in a quiet meal at home watching a television show that didn't suck. She grabbed a container of sushi rolls and a bottle of pinot gris before she headed to the checkout, stopping when the cover picture on a gossip magazine caught her eye.

The latest up-and-coming Hollywood heartthrob, Jasonsomething, was captured doing a back handspring in front of his new girlfriend, a sexy lingerie model. The headline read, *He flipped for her!*

"I wish someone would flip for me," she said to herself before grabbing the magazine and adding it to her purchases. "Might as well read about someone else's love life."

She hummed the entire walk home and up three flights of stairs, her key in her hand so she wouldn't have to struggle to find it. Brianna halted at her landing. The front door stood ajar. The humming stopped, and her cheery feeling vanished. Setting down her groceries outside the door, she dug out the pepper spray from her bag and poked her head inside the apartment.

Panic flowed through Brianna as she entered. The first thing she noticed was that the living room had been stripped bare. The ratty couch Naomi parked her butt on all the time was missing, a dusty rectangle the only evidence it had been there. The cords for the cable snaked out of the wall, waiting to be plugged into a television that was no longer there. Nail holes decorated the walls, as well as faded squares and circles, remnants of objects taken. A dust bunny rolled past Brianna, following the floorboards and settling down in the corner.

She inched her way to the kitchen and saw it was barren as well. The cabinet doors were open, revealing empty spaces where the secondhand pots, pans, and plates once sat. Another door lay on the floor, ripped off and discarded. The dented cans of meat, vegetables, and packaged dinners she'd purchased on sale at the bargain store had vanished as well.

Not believing her eyes, she continued to the hallway. Hope held out that the thief had stopped with the living room and kitchen and her bedroom would be intact, but as she passed Naomi's room, she saw it had been emptied too.

Brianna closed her eyes. "Why is this happening?"

Dreading what she would see, she opened her eyes and shuffled to her room. Her mattress sat on the floor, devoid of sheets, while the rest of her furniture was gone. The philoden-dron her mother had given her the last time she visited was on its side, dirt spilling onto the floor. Brianna picked up the plant like a shield and walked around, looking for clues to explain what had happened.

She checked the closet and found most of her clothes gone, empty hangers emphasizing what used to be. Her collection of high heels was missing, but a pair of old tennis shoes peeked out from one corner. Whoever cleaned out the place must not have seen them. Or decided they weren't worth taking.

Brianna felt sick as she approached her mattress. She knew the money would be gone, but she had to see for herself. Setting down the philodendron, Brianna slid her hand under the bottom corner of the bed. Nothing. Holding up the corner, she bent down to look. Brianna saw two loose $20 bills, but the rest of her windfall was missing.

Rather than retrieve the money, Brianna dropped the mattress and put her head in her hands. Tears fell between her fingers. She had nothing now. It wasn't like she'd had a lot before, but whoever had done this took what little she had.

It wasn't fair.

She let herself cry for a few minutes before she stumbled to the bathroom. She turned on the cold water in the sink and splashed her face. The water jolted her and soothed her eyes, but it didn't banish the shock of what had happened. It did make her realize that the thief had also taken the hand towel.

Brianna dried her face the best she could with her sleeve before she looked at her reflection in the mirror. She clenched her jaw and observed the face staring back at her. Puffy eyes looked out over a red nose. It reminded her of the day she found out Doug had stolen her savings. A day she discovered how weak and vulnerable she was. A day she swore would never happen again.

As she cursed herself under her breath, she noticed a

piece of paper taped to the back of the bathroom door. Brianna whirled around and yanked it down. She felt dizzy as the blood drained from her head, and she sank to the bathroom floor after reading the note.

Brianna,
Thanks for being a great roommate. I never would have guessed when I set this up a few months ago that it would be this profitable. Most of the time I only get some clothes and crappy furniture. But the money under the mattress? That made my day.
Best,
Naomi

Brianna balled up the note and threw it across the room. She didn't want to admit it, but her mother was right. She was a bad judge of character, apparently with women as well as men.

She let herself have another good cry. When she was empty of tears and emotion, she washed her face again—this time letting it air-dry—and headed back to the living room. As she assessed the situation, she considered her options. The apartment lease was in her name and rent was paid for the month, as were the utilities. Her renter's insurance should cover the loss of her belongings, although all her receipts and records were missing as well. The nightmare of fixing this mess made her want to cry again, but her stomach grumbled, reminding her of the takeout she'd brought home.

Wandering to the front door for her food, she gave a silent prayer of thanks that the sushi came with chopsticks and the wine bottle had a screw top. She plunked on the floor of the living room while she ate her dinner and drank wine straight from the bottle. Brianna tossed the fashion magazine in the corner with the dust bunny. It would be a long time before she could afford any designer clothes.

Once she was sufficiently full from dinner, Brianna called

the police. The dispatcher promised to send an officer as soon as possible, but Brianna knew it could be hours before someone showed up. She wandered through the apartment again, careful not to touch anything.

The second pass revealed that Naomi had left her a broom, a dustpan, a couple blankets, a towel, a stack of paper plates, and an odd assortment of clothes scattered around the apartment.

Back in the living room, Brianna lowered herself to the floor and lay down. "This isn't the end of the world. I've gotten through worse."

She closed her eyes as she calmed herself. Crying wasn't going to help anything. She was doing the right thing. After she had a police report, she could file it with the insurance company. At least Doug's behavior had taught her to insure everything.

―――――――――――――――

Chapter 7

―――――――――――――――

The next morning at work, Brianna groaned when she reached for the ringing telephone. Her entire body was sore and stiff, a sign she should have taken Shelby up on her offer to stay in her guest room. But it was late by the time the police showed up to take the incident report. She was too keyed up to sleep. Instead, she cleaned her apartment, which didn't take long due to the lack of furniture. Then she'd run down to the laundry room to wash the smelly blankets and towels that had been left behind and didn't get to bed until well after midnight.

She summoned what energy she had to sound professional when she answered the phone. "Good morning. Dunderblatt and Watson. How can I help you?"

"Brianna? Is that you?"

She recognized Carl Raeburn's voice, and a genuine smile spread across her face. She didn't understand why Raeburn put up with Alex's antics, but she didn't care. He was the only one of Alex's clients she enjoyed working with.

"Yes, Mr. Raeburn. It's me. How are you this morning?"

"Better than you from the sound of your voice. You sound tired. Everything okay?"

She nodded her head, which earned her a shooting pain down her neck. "Yes. Bad night's sleep is all." Not wanting to discuss the situation, Brianna asked, "What can I help you with?"

"I'm still waiting on the contract for the Brick Hallow residence. Do you know where it is?"

Sighing in frustration, Brianna put her head into her hand, which sent another sharp pain into one shoulder. If she didn't need the money, she'd be tempted to go home sick after this call. As it was, she didn't have a choice.

"I'm sorry about the contract. It's ready to go. It was on Alex's desk last I saw it." Which meant it was still on the desk, probably under a mountain of crap by now. "Let me see if I can find out what he did with it. Can I call you back?"

"Why don't you put me on hold? I don't mind waiting. You've got some good hold music these days. I assume you're behind that."

Brianna sat up a little straighter. She had nudged Alex to upgrade the music and message on their phones. Raeburn was the first person to say anything about it.

"Yes, that was me." It was nice to be recognized for doing something right occasionally. "Give me a few minutes to figure this out." She stabbed the hold button with her finger and heard a crack. Brianna looked down to see a chip in her nail polish. "Great. One more thing."

Doubting she could spare the money for a manicure anytime soon, she headed from her desk to Alex's office. He hadn't bothered to come in today. Apparently, his date the previous evening had gone long, and his morning text to her simply said, *Handle things.*

Brianna opened the office door and gasped when she saw the state of Alex's desk. Papers covered the surface, a dozen coffee cups sticking up like towers. The trash can overflowed with energy drink cans and protein bar wrappers.

Faced with the mess, Brianna went straight to the break

room and got several trash bags. She scrounged under the sink and found a pair of rubber gloves as well.

"I should get hazmat pay for this," she mumbled to herself as she made her way back to the office.

She emptied the trash, then shoved the coffee cups into the trash bag. She found some takeout containers from the Chinese place down the street and threw them out, the smell telling her nothing edible was left inside. Once she had removed the biohazardous materials, Brianna sorted through papers, stacking things she recognized, throwing junk mail into the trash bag, and averting her eyes when she unearthed several sleazy magazines with women in various stages of undress.

She hit pay dirt under the magazines, though. Raeburn's contract was hidden there, stained by grease from the Chinese food but signed by Alex. With a sigh of relief, Brianna left Alex's office, peeled off the gloves, and fed the paperwork into the scanner. She ran to the kitchen to wash her hands, then dashed back to her desk, where she emailed the completed scan to the client. Wishing she could take a shower as well, Brianna picked up the phone and pressed the button to reconnect with the client.

"Mr. Raeburn, I found the contract. It was signed but hadn't been returned to you. I emailed you a copy. Did you get it yet?"

The man said, "I should deal with you going forward. You get things done."

Brianna basked in the compliment for a second, then returned to reality. She needed this job. The client might like the fact that she went above and beyond the call of duty, but Alex might not be happy when he discovered she knew about his magazine collection.

"Thank you. Feel free to call or email me if you need anything else."

"I will. Definitely."

She started to put the phone done when she heard Raeburn add,

"If it weren't for you, Dunderblatt would go belly-up. You deserve a raise."

"Thank you, sir. I appreciate it."

"I'm serious. If you ever get tired of Alex, give me a call. I could use someone like you in my office."

Brianna paused. She didn't know what Raeburn did other than buy dilapidated houses, but considering her situation, it wouldn't hurt to find some different options. A backup job could come in handy.

"What do you do, Mr. Raeburn?"

"Officially, I'm retired. Sold my consulting company to the highest bidder about five years ago. Bought a nice beachfront property in Saint Kitts and lowered my handicap index to 6.4. I'm a threat in the club tournaments these days."

She frowned. She had no idea what a handicap index was, but she did know she couldn't afford to move internationally. *Been there, done that.* But she was still curious what Raeburn was doing with the houses he bought.

"If you're out of the country, why buy property here in Vegas?"

Raeburn laughed. "Great question. I lasted about a year before I got stir-crazy and started looking for something to do. My wife has volunteered for a women's shelter here in town for years. She's always explaining how hard it is for women— especially mothers—to find safe, inexpensive housing. I started a property management company tailored to fill those needs. I buy apartments, houses, whatever I can find. My friend, Jared, and his company fix them up. My wife handles promotion to area shelters and support groups. I have a property manager who rents out and manages the properties since we still go back and forth to the island."

Brianna sat back in her chair. Never in a million years did she expect to learn that one of Alex's clients was philanthropically inclined. It didn't match with the narcissistic, chauvinistic man her boss was.

"Does Alex know what you do?"

The question was out of her mouth before she could stop herself. It didn't matter to her boss what people did with their purchases so long as he made a commission on it.

"I told him a while back," Raeburn chuckled, "but he said Jared and I were crazy. He explained how we were leaving money on the table. In the end, who cares? He called me a chump, but he's still making easy money selling me these houses."

Brianna could imagine those words coming out of Alex's mouth. He thought about no one but himself. Just like her former roommate and her last boyfriend. It was nice to know not everyone was a self-centered narcissist.

"I think what you're doing is wonderful. People need help to get back on their feet, and if someone doesn't help them, how would they manage it?" She wondered what Alex would think if she considered Raeburn's offer before shaking her head. No use wondering about things that weren't going to happen.

"I'm serious, Brianna. Call me if you want to talk more about a position. I'm sure my property manager, Gwen, wouldn't mind having some help, especially someone as organized as you. You've got my number."

As she went about her day, Brianna wondered what it would be like to work somewhere she made a difference and was treated professionally. The clientele at Raeburn's office had to be better than those she encountered here, and she would be working for a worthy cause. But she liked selling real estate, and that wasn't what Raeburn needed. Better to stick with the plan than make another change.

Chapter 8

Brianna found herself sitting on the hard floor of her empty apartment several nights later. She had twenty minutes to kill while she waited for her laundry to finish drying. It was getting old doing laundry every other night, but until she got reimbursed by the insurance company she had no choice, as she only had a few outfits left to wear.

She'd spent the last of her money on a few pieces of clothing for work, a beanbag chair, some food, and other essential items. She planned to buy replacement furnishings with the check from insurance, but the company representative said it could take thirty to ninety days.

"My fault for going with the cheaper company and not reading the fine print," she told Philomena, her philodendron. She knew it was stupid to name it, but she needed to call it something other than "Plant," especially since she carried it with her from room to room. She didn't feel alone when she had another living thing in the same room with her. "Are you as bored as I am sitting around here waiting for"—she waved her hands in the air—"something? I don't even know what. Maybe I should try the casino again."

With no money to spare, Brianna crawled to the beanbag

and sank into it. The quiet bothered her. As much as she had hated Naomi's choice of television, the constant noise had been comforting. Without a television or stereo, the only sound left was her own voice and podcasts she played from her cell phone.

So far, her favorite show discussed women's independence. The host argued women should be single and self-sufficient. "Why rely on anyone but yourself?" was the podcaster's sign-off at the end of each episode.

Brianna stared at the ceiling while she pondered that question. Because she didn't want to rely on herself. She liked being in a relationship, which explained why the last few months hadn't been her finest. Sharing an apartment had helped. She might not have a man, but she did have someone to come home to each night.

If the podcaster was right, as long as she was more self-reliant, her bad choices in men wouldn't hurt as much. Self-reliance sounded better than giving up men. It was a logical thing to do, but it sounded as appetizing as eating crickets.

The fantasy of Prince Charming showing up on her doorstep, offering her the perfect life, was a long shot, but stranger things had happened. Doug had won the lottery. She had won a huge slot machine payout. Sometimes gambles paid off.

But the truth was, even when she did put in the hard work, life still found a way to take her down a notch. How was she supposed to know Alex's office didn't hold any long-term benefit for her, or that Naomi would be a conniving frenemy? That's why she couldn't give up hope that someone or something would change her life.

The timer on her phone rang, signaling her laundry was finished. She waved at Philomena. "I'll be right back." She was lonely, not desperate. The plant didn't need to join her as she walked down four flights of stairs to retrieve her clothes.

When she entered the laundry room, Brianna saw that the

doors on all the washers and dryers were open. She hurried to the dryer where she'd put her clothes less than an hour ago. She ran her hand around the empty tumbler, tears threatening to spill. It was bad enough she had no furniture left. Why did someone need to take her clothes as well?

Brianna searched every corner of the laundry room before she gave up. She trudged back upstairs and flopped down on the beanbag. A loud pop startled her as the white beans from inside shot upward and then showered down on her. Her only piece of living room furniture had sprung a leak.

She couldn't stop the tears this time, letting them roll down her cheeks unchecked. She had nothing. No roommate. No money. No clothes. No beanbag. No boyfriend.

What else could go wrong?

"No, don't answer that," she mumbled to the empty room. "I can't take anything else. Please let one good thing happen this week. I've had enough bad stuff for the rest of the year."

When she was calm, Brianna brushed the white beads from her face, dried her tears with the edge of her T-shirt, and stood up. She didn't have any other choice but to clean up the mess and fix the beanbag.

Brianna swept up the little pellets and put them in a trash bag, double- and triple-bagging it. She stuffed the beanbag into a trash bag as well and then arranged them on the floor like a chair and footrest. She was in no position to throw away anything. She'd make do with what she had.

Maybe it was time to find a new job. That was more of a guarantee of income than gambling. She could always call Raeburn. After they'd talked, he emailed her an offer letter, including salary and bonus information. It seemed forward of him, but it was good to know her options.

With the new job, she could make ends meet and do a little catch-up. She'd even have money in the bank when the insurance check came through.

A change of apartment made sense as well. This place was

too big for her on her own, and she didn't want to spend all her money on rent. Not since she needed to buy new clothes now.

Moving with nothing would be an interesting experience. It reminded her of movies when a character showed up at a hotel with no luggage, only a black trash bag. She might have several trash bags, although the beanbag wasn't something she wanted to move into her new space. It would be better to start from scratch.

She settled back and surveyed the apartment. It wasn't much, but it was hers. This was the first place she had lived in Las Vegas. Truth be told, she wasn't ready to let go of it yet. Plus, her lease wasn't up for another six months.

The only thing she could do right now was give up on finding a man.

She slumped into the beanbag as her mother's words echoed in her head: "You've got to stop looking for the wrong thing in the wrong person."

Thankful she didn't have to admit to her mother that she was right, Brianna crossed her arms over her chest and pouted. It wasn't like she was breaking up with a boyfriend. She was only letting go of the idea of having one. It wouldn't be forever. Only until she could get her real estate license and her finances in order.

She could do this. She wasn't giving up on herself and her dream. Things hadn't gone as planned, but if she quit now, she might miss out on her dreams in the long run.

Staying at Alex's office and in this apartment was the right thing to do. Something good would come from it. She knew it.

Chapter 9

A knock at the door startled her. While she doubted her "something good" had shown up so fast, whoever was at the door would be a distraction. She rolled off the beanbag, picking white pellets from her sleeve as she walked to the door.

She didn't know anyone in her building other than Naomi, and she doubted her former roommate would knock after robbing her blind, so Brianna peeked through the security hole. A man stood there holding a laundry basket. She recognized one of the shirts. It was hers.

Brianna flung the door open. "What are you doing with my clothes?"

Excited to see her things, she stepped out into the hall and took the basket. She set it on the ground, checking to see if all her stuff was there. Relieved to know that one of her problems was solved, she looked up to thank him and froze.

Shaking her head, she stood up and stared at the man in front of her. Of course the universe would send Mr. Tall-Dark-and-Handsome to her front door the minute she gave up on men. A pair of ice-blue eyes stared at her over cheeks partially covered by a five-o'clock shadow. His lips turned up on the sides, and she bit her lip to keep from sighing.

Brianna blinked a few times before she realized he was asking her a question. "What did you say?"

"I asked if you know how many women live in this building?"

Brianna's brows furrowed. "That's a random question."

"Maybe."

He shrugged. His biceps flexed, and Brianna admired the way his muscles moved. He spent some time in the gym, which made her regret her decision to avoid men for a while.

Before she could come up with a response that was pleasant but not flirty, he continued.

"So far, I've met twelve while I was trying to reunite you with your clothes. I was ready to throw in the towel, metaphorically speaking, although I did notice there is a towel in this hamper." He pointed to the laundry basket. "I'm sorry about the mix-up. I sent my daughter to grab our laundry, and she took everything from both dryers. We've had a talk about how this will never happen again. And, as a show of good faith, I'd like you to keep the laundry basket."

The relief of getting her clothes back brought tears to Brianna's eyes. How was it possible that a guy this cute would have a daughter who stole her clothes? Maybe it was a trick. He could be a psychopathic murderer.

She debated about asking for his ID but said instead, "Thank you. For the clothes and the basket. I needed a new one."

His eyes grew wide as he peeked over her shoulder. "Looks like you need more than a laundry basket. Are you waiting for a moving truck? Ours got rerouted when we moved here. We lived in sleeping bags for a week before it showed. I still have the bruises to prove it." He rubbed his back. "If you flip the basket upside down, you'll get a table. Maybe your plant would like that."

The non sequitur response relaxed her. If this guy was a murderer, he was an amusing one.

He held out his hand. "I'm Kevin Ramsey in 8C. My daughter, the would-be laundry thief, is Rosemary. We moved in a few weeks ago."

She shook his hand and started to introduce herself, but a warm, tingly sensation raced through her body. Biting her lip, she reminded herself that she was no longer interested in men. Besides, Kevin Ramsey had a daughter, which meant there was a wife, ex-wife, or girlfriend in there somewhere.

"Again, sorry about the laundry. I promise it won't happen again."

Brianna cleared her throat. Before she knew what she was saying, she blurted out, "Thank you for bringing these back. It's been a tough week, and I wasn't sure how I was going to manage without clothes. And I could definitely use the table. My roommate stole all my stuff. I've been dumped twice this week and my boss is an ass. This is the nicest thing that's happened in a while."

A look of surprise crossed Kevin's face, and Brianna cringed. A simple thank you would have been enough, and maybe she could have a friend in the building. Too late now. She'd embarrassed herself with her word vomit.

"If I hadn't seen it for myself, I would have thought you were exaggerating. What do you need? A cot or a sleeping bag? I have a bunch of stuff in storage I could loan you."

Kevin's generosity threw Brianna for a loop. Shelby's offer to help had made sense, but Kevin didn't know her at all. She'd accused him of stealing her clothes and complained about her horrible week, and he still volunteered his assistance.

She shook her head. "You don't even know me. Why would you offer to help?"

Kevin looked at his feet for a few seconds before meeting her gaze. "It's good to help people. Especially after stealing their laundry."

She thought he wanted to say something else, but he stood there waiting for her to make a request.

"Well, if you have a coffeepot, or even a spare pan I could boil water in, that would be great."

A gleam sparkled in Kevin's eye. "I can do that. The apartment kitchen is tiny; most of our stuff is still boxed up. How about a skillet? I've got lots of cooking gadgets you could borrow."

Brianna nodded. "That would be great. Naomi wiped me out. She even took the napkins."

Kevin laughed. "I've got those too. Rosemary is a messy eater, so I buy in bulk. Give me half an hour to dig things out and I'll be back."

He turned and walked down the hall when Brianna remembered something.

"Hey, Kevin?"

When Kevin turned to face her, Brianna noticed the smile on his face seemed to be drooping, as if he thought she had changed her mind. She also admired how handsome he was. His light-brown hair curled around his ears. He could use a haircut, she thought, as her fingers itched to smooth it in place.

She tamped down her hormones and told herself it was better to be appreciative of his help than to get romantically involved. He was being a good neighbor.

"It's really no problem. I don't mind," he said encouragingly.

She smiled. "I wasn't going to protest. I was going to tell you my name."

His cheeks flushed, and he stammered, "That might be good. Yeah."

"My name is Brianna. It's nice to meet you, Kevin."

Kevin walked back down the hall and put out his hand again. Brianna hesitated, still not sure why someone would be nice to her.

Get over yourself, she thought, and she shook his hand.

"It's a pleasure. Sorry again for my daughter's thievery, but she's still adjusting since her mom died."

Chapter 10

Brianna's arm froze mid-shake. She couldn't decide whether she should be happy that Kevin was single or horrified that she was capitalizing on someone's loss. But he saved her from having to make a decision.

"It's okay. Linda passed away four years ago. Breast cancer. Rosemary was eight."

She wanted to say something rather than stand there looking like a curiosity junkie, but instead of speaking, instinct took over. Brianna pulled Kevin into a hug.

The gesture must have surprised Kevin as much as it did her, because he turned slightly. His shoulder collided with her sternum, and her cleavage gave his upper arm a squeeze. Embarrassed by the result of her action and hoping he didn't think she was hitting on him, she pulled back but couldn't completely separate, since Kevin held onto her hand.

"That's the nicest thing anyone has done when I've told them about Linda. Most people end the conversation as fast as possible and never talk to me again. I'm a bit of an over-sharer, if you hadn't already figured that out."

He finally dropped her hand and started down the hall

again. At the top of the stairs, he turned and called, "I'll be back."

Brianna stood there and watched him disappear. When he was gone, she turned back into her apartment and closed the door behind her. Shaking her head, she noticed that not only were her clothes clean but they were also neatly folded, even her pajamas. Her socks were tucked together in matching pairs, and her underwear was folded in thirds, reminding her of an origami swan her mother used to make for her when she was little.

It said a lot about Kevin. He cared about the details. He made time for them, even though he was both mother and father to his daughter. It was proof that there were good men in the world. Kevin might even qualify for Prince Charming if he came through with a coffeepot.

Brianna carried her clothes to her room. She put everything away as best as she could before returning to the living room. It only took a few seconds to reorganize her meager amount of furniture to include the laundry basket coffee table.

Wanting to be a good host, she went to the kitchen and searched for something she could serve as a snack. She arranged half a box of sandwich cookies on a paper plate and filled two paper cups with water. Brianna took the refreshments and put them on her makeshift table, then eased herself onto the beanbag.

She closed her eyes while she waited for Kevin to return.

What would it be like to lose your wife or husband and raise a daughter alone? All Brianna's relationships had ended poorly, but no one had died. How would that make her feel?

She imagined what it would have been like if she and Doug had gotten married. They'd talked about it, but Doug would never commit. That should have been a clue, but she was infatuated. At least until he stole her money. His deceit had left her angry, and she didn't miss him at all. In fact, she hoped to never see him again.

That couldn't be how Kevin felt.

He'd planned to be with Linda forever. They had a daughter and everything. From his reaction, she knew he still missed her. What if Rosemary looked like Linda? How much pain would it cause to see the image of the love of your life every day and know you would never see her again?

That's when it hit her, and Brianna's eyelids flew open.

Nothing was guaranteed.

The epiphany forced Brianna out of the beanbag. She raced to the kitchen to find her cell phone. Meeting Kevin was the sign she needed. It was time to try something new.

She tapped out an email to Raeburn, letting him know she was interested in a position at his company. She hit send before she could change her mind, then tossed her phone on the kitchen counter and returned to the beanbag.

Thinking about what she had done, Brianna's heart raced. What if Raeburn had been kidding and didn't need any help? Maybe he was being polite, and she had misinterpreted his intentions. She dropped her head into her hands and closed her eyes. She did this to herself all the time. When would she learn she couldn't depend on other people?

"This is stupid," she mumbled to herself. "You made an effort. It doesn't matter if you get this job or not. At least you tried."

Her cell phone chimed, signaling an incoming email. When Brianna attempted to get out of the beanbag, the plastic trash bag stuck to her skin and held her in place. She heard the phone chime again. In her haste, she rolled to the side to break the connection between her and the bag. She was rewarded with a ripping sound and another flurry of white pellets.

"Not again." She sighed and left the cleaning for later as she retrieved her phone. She was surprised to see an email from Raeburn.

I'm happy to have you aboard. When can you start?

Relief washed over her as she realized she hadn't misunderstood. Excitement followed when she read what she would be making at her new job. Fear took charge when she thought about a start date.

She didn't know how Alex would react to the news. He might kick her out immediately or he might want her to stay for two weeks. There was no way of knowing until she talked to him. Which was another issue. He may or may not be in the office the next morning. She crinkled her nose in frustration. She didn't want to deal with her unpredictable boss.

Brianna composed an email back, hoping her gamble paid off.

I need to give a two-week notice to Mr. Dunderblatt, then I can start immediately. If he doesn't want the notice, I could start as early as the day after tomorrow. Can I let you know after I speak with him?

She sent the response and received an immediate reply.

I appreciate your situation. Email me after you talk with Alex. I've got plenty to get you started. Looking forward to having you on the team!

Thrilled with the news, Brianna relaxed. Now she had a new job and a nice neighbor who was going to let her borrow a few things until she could afford to replace them. As she considered her good luck, she wondered if she should offer to help Kevin with Rosemary. Maybe she would be better with older kids than she had been with Doug's small children.

She rolled her eyes when she remembered the disaster of the inappropriate Christmas gifts a few years back. The sequined halter top and matching short shorts had looked cute in the magazine but, apparently, weren't appropriate for seven-year-old girls. And seven-year-old boys didn't need custom-built motorcycles either.

The door creaked open, and Brianna shook the memories out of her head.

"I wasn't sure what exactly you needed. Here's a bunch of stuff," Kevin said. He held a cardboard container in his hands, and she saw another one sitting outside her apartment. "Anything you don't need I'll take back. Or if you need something else, let me know. I have lots to choose from."

She bent down in the hall and groaned at the weight of the container. "What do you have in here? And how did you carry all this down four flights of stairs?"

"Hold on! Let me help you," Kevin said as he set down the stuff he was holding and turned back to help her. Brianna's load lightened as Kevin grabbed hold of the box and nodded to the kitchen. "This one's full of kitchen stuff. Can you make it over there?"

She nodded and managed to make it to the threshold of the kitchen before her arms gave out. Her side of the container tilted downward, out of Kevin's grip, and slammed into the floor. Brianna cringed as she waited for what would come next.

A loud rapping on the floor filled the room, followed by, "Keep it down up there!"

Kevin grinned. "Do you spend a lot of time with that neighbor? She sounds lovely."

Brianna giggled before slapping her hand over her face.

Kevin continued as if nothing was wrong. "She reminds me of the woman on my floor with the chihuahua that doesn't like anyone. Including its owner. Don't know why anyone would keep a dog like that. It's not even cute. It's always dressed up in a red-and-yellow shirt that reminds me of Stewie from *Family Guy*. The dog's head isn't that big, but it *is* shaped like a football."

He pulled several pots and pans from the box and showed them to her. "I'm a firm believer in cast iron. That's why it's heavy."

She stood there as he unpacked what looked like a complete kitchen and set it on the counter. Brianna still couldn't believe the generosity of this man, whom she had met only because his daughter had stolen her clothes. That thought prompted her next question.

"Where's your daughter?" Brianna asked. "I'd like to meet her."

Kevin shook his head as he took out a coffeepot and filled it with water. "She's shy, so she stayed home. Although she did want you to know she's sorry." He set the coffeepot on the counter before rummaging through the supplies he'd brought. He found a can of coffee, scooped out the appropriate amount, and poured it into the machine. Then he plugged it in and asked, "What time do you want your coffee ready in the morning?"

Brianna shrugged. "Seven, I guess."

He tapped some buttons on the machine and turned back to her. "Okay. All programmed for tomorrow. I'll let you unload the rest. Rosemary's probably wondering what's taking so long." He took a step toward the kitchen door, then stopped. "To be honest, the therapist thinks Rosemary likes to be alone because her mom died when she was young. She's always been more comfortable on her own than she is with other people. Linda got her to interact more before she got sick, but once Linda was bedridden . . ."

Kevin's voice trailed off, and Brianna fought the urge to give him another hug. One hug was okay. Two would be creepy.

He must have sensed her inner dilemma because he gave her a sad smile and said, "Rosemary wouldn't leave her side. We're working on it. Anyway, glad I could help tonight."

With a quick wave, Kevin let himself out.

Brianna wrapped her arms around herself. Nothing could have prepared her for the evening's outcome, and she was both happy and sad. On a positive note, she had kitchen supplies. But she had to face Alex tomorrow. And she didn't even want to consider how she felt about Rosemary and Kevin's situation.

Instead of dwelling on things, Brianna opened the other box Kevin had left. She pulled out the newspaper stuffed around the items to protect them. She tossed it on the ground before the masthead grabbed her attention.

The Gazette, the newspaper from Glen Valley, Doug's hometown, stared up at her.

She grabbed the paper, curious to see what had been happening in the small town. Brianna skimmed through the headlines, nodding as she recognized Cynthia Anderson's byline. The reporter was known for her willingness to write a less-than-flattering article if the situation called for it. After she read the article, Brianna knew Cynthia hadn't lost her touch. The reporter railed against an upsurge in homelessness for women and children, which affirmed Brianna's decision to work for Raeburn.

If Mr. Raeburn wants to branch out, I'll suggest Glen Valley.

Another column and byline caught her attention. *Planning Your Dream Wedding*, by Helene Shaw, should have surprised her more, but it made sense. Doug's ex-mother-in-law enjoyed giving people suggestions. Why not write them up in a column?

Brianna shook her head. Glen Valley wasn't a place she had liked visiting, but it was interesting to hear how things were going there. She made a mental note to ask Kevin how he got the paper as she headed to bed. She needed her rest to deal with Alex.

Chapter 11

Cynthia stretched her arms over her head and yawned. Her computer told her it was 11:30 p.m., and her stomach told her she had missed dinner again. She'd pushed herself the last few weeks, following up on the homelessness article she'd written. It made her sick to think about the women and children who didn't have a comfortable bed to sleep in at night. If she didn't live with her mother, she would have given her room to one of the struggling mothers she'd interviewed.

But she didn't live on her own, and the countdown was on. She had three months before her mother's deadline. Three months to find some place to live, or she would be homeless too.

Cynthia pushed the thought from her mind and pulled up the draft of Helene's latest edition to her wedding column, *Planning Your Dream Wedding*. When Cynthia suggested the idea to Helene after the woman had applied for *The Gazette's* Wedding of the Year contest, she didn't expect Helene to greet it with much gusto, but she had. Helene thrived on putting copious amounts of detail into each of the weekly articles.

So far, Helene had written about choosing a venue,

selecting a caterer, and interviewing a DJ. This week's topic was how to pick the perfect wedding gown, and Helene's description on how to match a bride's body to a dress was both helpful and humorous. Cynthia glowed over the recognition her editor gave her in the morning meeting.

"Stroke of genius to have that woman write the column. Especially now she's the talk of the town."

The haze of happiness softened the reality of the press release that sat on her desk. Her editor thought she could work more magic and get details behind the Miller Agency, the company that was responsible for revitalizing Glen Valley's riverfront area and stealing away Sara Shaw, a Glen Valley native. Now the agency was involved in some philanthropic work, and Cynthia's boss wanted to do a story on it.

"Not only does it play off the homelessness angle you covered, it's a 'local girl makes it big' angle. She's in Chicago, working for Jared Hughes, a big-time land use and zoning lawyer who happens to be a college football legend." Cynthia knew her editor was a football fan, and she worried he might ask her to get Hughes's autograph while she got the story. "Try to get a quote from Jared as well."

Hoping Sara didn't hold a grudge for the article she'd written a while back about the Miller Agency's work in Glen Valley, Cynthia typed up an email.

Hi, Sara. It's Cynthia Anderson from The Gazette in Glen Valley. I heard about the project the Miller Agency is working on in Las Vegas and wanted to schedule some time to talk with you. This would make an impressive article. We could run it next to your mom's next wedding column, which, by the way, is the most-read column in the paper. Your mom is doing a great job.

Cynthia considered deleting the part about Helene. She knew Helene and Sara had their differences, and one of the reasons Sara had moved to Chicago was because of Helene. Cynthia hoped her compliment didn't work against her. She needed this interview.

Please give me a call back to discuss the low-rent apartments you're renovating for women and children.

She hit send and reread the press release. In addition to Sara's name, a Gwen Martin was listed. Gwen wasn't a former Glen Valley resident and wouldn't have the same name recognition Sara had. But if Sara didn't get back to her, Cynthia needed someone to interview. She entered the URL for the website listed with Gwen's contact information and confirmed many of the details from the press release. Then she clicked on the Contacts page.

Call it human nature, but Cynthia liked having a picture of who she was communicating with in front of her. She gazed at Gwen Martin's picture. An austere expression stared back at her. Sleek, dark hair surrounded Gwen's pale face. Bright-red lipstick popped out from the center of the picture.

Cynthia sighed. Gwen reminded her of her mother, Cybil. Cold, calculating, and in control.

She pushed back from her chair and walked around the room. Cynthia needed to focus on this story, but the issue with her mother and the living arrangements wouldn't go away. Walking to the whiteboard mounted on the wall, she brainstormed her options.

Move out.

Buy the house from Mom.

Ask Mom to rent a pottery studio somewhere else.

Of the three options, moving out was the only logical one. Real estate was in high demand. Finding someplace she liked would be difficult. Her mother didn't want to sell. Cybil called this her "toes up" house: her mother planned to be here until she died. There weren't many options to rent studio space, either. Glen Valley recently got its first drive-thru coffee shop, thanks to Betty's Coffee Bar. But Cybil would need to go a town or two over if she wanted something large enough to put in a kiln and lots of workspace.

Cynthia turned from the whiteboard and went back to her

computer. Speculating on her mother's motivations wasn't going to solve anything. If she wanted to get some sleep tonight, she needed to email this Gwen Martin and set up a time to talk. With a plan in place, the knot in her stomach loosened a bit, and Cynthia settled down to type her final email of the evening.

Chapter 12

Brianna woke the next morning to the smell of fresh-brewed coffee.

"Thank heaven for programmable coffeepots!"

She stretched her arms over her head and yawned. She felt well rested for the first time since her furniture had disappeared. Whether it was the coffee or the prospect that today might be her last day in Alex's office, she didn't know or care.

She dressed in her neatly folded clothes. She envied Rosemary and Kevin's mad folding abilities. For the first time in ages, her pants boasted a crisp crease down the front, and her shirt's arms weren't wrinkled. Brianna considered asking them for their secret. If a twelve-year-old could do it, why couldn't she?

The coffee revved her up even more. Kevin knew his coffee, that was for sure. She poured herself a to-go cup and, as an afterthought, poured a second one as a peace offering to Alex. It never hurt to butter up her boss. She grabbed her purse and the coffees before heading out the door. Brianna hoped to run into Kevin on the way out, but since she'd never run into him before last night, she doubted their schedules overlapped. When she didn't see him in the lobby, she pretended it didn't matter and made her way out to the sidewalk.

The walk to work usually relaxed her, but Brianna struggled to keep her nerves in check as she got closer to the office. Handing in her notice made her jittery. She didn't know how Alex would react. It was hard to tell if he would be logical or hungover on any given day.

It turned out she had to wait until after lunch to talk to Alex. When he finally showed up for the day, he looked tired but not hungover. That was a good sign. She let him get settled in his office before she picked up the list of things she needed to discuss with him. Her leaving was the last item, and along with it was a resignation letter she'd spent the morning polishing.

She reheated the cup of coffee she'd brought for Alex, then knocked on his office door. Brianna waited to be called in. Her stomach clenched, which she hoped was a sign of excitement but was more likely nerves.

"Come in," Alex called, and she pushed open the door. Her boss sat behind his desk, his hands clasped in front of him, like he had been waiting for her to knock. "I wondered how long it would take you."

She paused. *He knows something is up. Did Mr. Raeburn tell him?*

"Come on in. I don't have all day. Especially since you've got something you want to tell me, don't you?"

She frowned. "Why do you say that?"

Alex pointed to his phone. "You copied me on your conversation with Carl last night." He leaned back in his chair and crossed his arms over his chest. "Is this office so bad that you want to go someplace else?"

Brianna's heart threatened to pop out of her chest. She wiped the beads of sweat that appeared on her forehead as she chastised herself for her error. Of course she would accidentally do something to alert Alex of her intentions.

Brianna glanced at Alex, relaxed back in his chair. He wasn't reacting the way she imagined he would. She expected screaming and yelling, not calm interrogation. She handed him his coffee, but when he didn't take it she put it down on his desk.

Make the best of the situation you got yourself in. You have some-where else to go anyway.

"I'd like to do more, to be honest. I am a real estate agent, and my goal is to get my license here in Nevada, remember?"

He nodded. "I know. I've seen you studying. If you're ready to take the exam, all you have to do is let me know. I said I would pay for it."

She fidgeted with the paper in her hands as guilt crept up on her. Should she have given Alex the benefit of the doubt? He had committed to the idea, but Brianna didn't think he had any intention of fulfilling his promise. Alex came in late all the time and seemed indifferent to how his clients treated her. If she had stood up for herself from the beginning, things might be different, but it was too late now.

Clearing her throat, she said, "Thank you. I appreciate the fact that you took a chance on me. But I'm not getting any closer to my license, and I've got another opportunity that will be better in line with my ultimate goal."

She bit her lip and waited to see Alex's reaction.

Alex picked up his coffee and took a sip. His eyebrows raised, and he gulped more down. "Wow. Why did you wait until your last day of work to display your coffee-making skills? I feel cheated."

She shrugged. "I brought this from home. Higher quality coffee tastes better."

Alex's eyes narrowed. "Now I'm cheap. Good to know. What else haven't you told me? Do you have a problem with how I run my office?"

She watched him drink his coffee as she mulled over what to say. If she told him how bad the place really was and how lucky he was that it was still running, it might upset him. He needed to know, though, that unless he made some changes in his business practices—more specifically his drinking practices—the firm would never do well.

Does he really want to hear that? No.

"You can run it any way you want. It's yours." She paused before adding, "And Watson's. But you are never going to get anywhere if you keep things up the way they are now. Unless you find someone who likes being a girl Friday."

Alex gave her a puzzled look.

"What's a girl Friday? It sounds illegal."

Shaking her head at his lack of vocabulary, she explained, "A girl Friday is a female office assistant who is expected to take care of everything. Like me. *I'm* your girl Friday."

He crushed his empty coffee cup and tossed it toward his trash can. When it missed, he laughed.

"So, my girl Friday would pick that up. Is that what you're saying?"

Sensing any meaningful conversation was over, she moved to the door, stepping around the cup on the floor. "I can give you two weeks' notice today and help you find someone to take my place. Or I can leave today and be out of your hair. Which do you prefer?"

Alex placed his forearms on the desk and leaned forward. "Tell me something. What is your ultimate goal?"

For the first time in a long time, she knew what she wanted. She wanted to take control of her life. That meant she needed to go where her boss was supportive and the clients weren't lecherous old men who made her uncomfortable.

"I want my Nevada real estate license, and eventually I'd like to run my own agency. The other position is more in line with what I want to do with my future." Brianna pushed down the image of Kevin's face. Now was not the time to think about her neighbor. "So, am I here for two weeks, or do I pack up my stuff?"

She prepared herself for a temper tantrum. Alex never gave in easily. The first week she'd worked for him, he broke the door off its hinges because a client had backed out of a deal. The client found a better property and brought it to Alex to close the deal, but the fit of anger had left an impression on Brianna. He wouldn't hurt her, but he could make things uncomfortable.

To her surprise, Alex nodded. "I get it. I'm being selfish by keeping you here. I knew the day I hired you that you were too good for this agency. Today can be your last day."

Her mouth dropped open and, for a few seconds, she was speechless. If she'd known he had this side to him, she might have considered sticking around. But it was too late now. She wasn't going to give up a great opportunity because Alex's compassion showed up for the first time.

"Thank you. I appreciate it," she said as she walked to the door. She paused as she considered how she would still have to work with Alex at Raeburn's office. It wouldn't hurt to leave on a good note. She owed him something for the way he was taking this. "If you want, I can write up a help wanted ad and get you a list of places to post it."

Alex's expression softened. She'd noticed he didn't know how to respond when people were nice. She felt a little sorry for him, although it was sort of his own fault.

"Thanks. That would be great." He came out from behind his desk, stuffing his hands in his pockets.

She nodded. "Consider it done."

She held out her hand. Alex reached out and shook it. For a second, Brianna thought he was going to pull her into a hug, which would be too much for her, but he didn't. Instead, he dropped her hand and let his own drop to his side.

"One last question."

Brianna stopped herself from rolling her eyes and said, "Shoot."

"Did you ever wonder if I really had a partner named John Watson?"

Brianna laughed. "The question crossed my mind. Since you're bringing it up, I assume there is no partner."

He shook his head. "My old man told me people trusted a partnership more than a sole proprietor. Even in the business world, to be a loner is bad news. Sort of like single men. We're all sharks."

Chapter 13

Brianna mulled over the shark comment as she prepared the job posting and made a list of places to submit it for Alex. She concluded that if single men were sharks, then single women were the prey. The idea sent shivers down her spine, even though it made sense. None of the men she dated had treated her like anything more than something to chase and discard, Doug included. Once he got what he wanted, he had tossed her aside like a day-old fish.

She'd made the right decision. Giving up on men was the best option.

With the rest of the afternoon ahead of her, Brianna ambled around downtown. She'd called Raeburn, hoping he would ask her to start this afternoon. His reply disappointed her.

"Gwen's out of the office today. Come in tomorrow at nine. Enjoy your afternoon off. You'll be busy soon enough."

She considered going home, but she didn't have furniture. Her back hurt at the prospect of lounging on the beanbag. Plus, if she went home, she'd be tempted to run up to 8C and thank Kevin again for his help. She had vowed off men, but Kevin was nice. Who could resist nice? And Rosemary would be home. Brianna knew she wasn't ready to meet the grieving tween yet.

Without realizing where she was going, Brianna found herself at the main entrance of the Diamond Casino and Hotel. She didn't want to gamble again, but she didn't have a lot of other options. She sat on the bench outside the casino and debated. The smart thing would be to head home and set out clothes for the rest of the week. She could do a few chapters of review for the real estate test on her cell phone, which wasn't ideal but would work.

What she really wanted was to relax and talk to a friend.

Brianna dug her cell phone out of her pocket and texted Shelby.

You have time to hang out today? I have a free afternoon.

"I thought you'd never ask."

Brianna's hand flew to her chest when she turned around to see Shelby standing behind her.

"How long have you been standing there?"

Shelby shrugged. "Since you sat down. I got off early. Things are slow today and the floor manager decided his girlfriend should get the hours over me. So, yeah, I'm free." She sat down next to Brianna. "The question is why are *you* free? Did Alex fire you?"

Brianna tilted her head to the side and frowned. "Why would you ask that?"

Shelby rummaged around in her purse and held up a package of gum. She offered Brianna a stick, then took one for herself. "I figured Alex finally crossed the line, and you punched him."

Brianna stopped unwrapping the gum and stared at her friend. "You know me too well."

Shelby popped the gum into her mouth and chewed. "Which is why I jumped to that conclusion. Besides, Alex is a complete imbecile. So, are you going to tell me what happened, or are we spending the afternoon searching for Prince Charming?"

Brianna rolled her eyes and grimaced as she watched Shelby chomp her gum. "Someone told me there was no such thing. Anyway, I didn't get fired. I quit. And I start my new job tomorrow."

Shelby looked at Brianna in surprise, a large bubble she had blown blocking half her face. Brianna couldn't resist. She stuck her finger into the bubble. It popped, allowing the sticky substance to ricochet back and stick to Shelby's face.

"I'm impressed." Shelby picked a string of gum off her nose. "Tell me about the new boss. Whose lackey are you going to be now?"

Brianna's cheeks warmed, but it was her own fault. Shelby knew her sordid employment history, and Alex was one of their favorite bashing points. It was Brianna's own fault that Shelby thought she would run from one bad boss to another.

"Actually, Mr. Raeburn is a great guy." Now was her chance to show Shelby that she wasn't a complete hack. "His company works with women's shelters to find low-rent apartments. A lot of the mothers can't afford to pay both rent and childcare. The apartments are affordable and safe enough for kids to live there."

Shelby pulled a piece of gum from her chin. "That's a huge step up from Alex, the man who nickel-and-dimed everything. How'd you find this job?"

Brianna watched Shelby pop the gum back in her mouth.

"Mr. Raeburn buys houses and apartments through Alex." Knowing that was as much praise as she was likely to get from Shelby, she changed the subject. "What do you want to do this afternoon?"

Pulling a compact from her purse, Shelby examined her face and nodded when she was satisfied she was now gum-free.

"We could check out the slot machines." She tilted her head to the casino. "Not here, though. Somewhere else."

Brianna shook her head. "I can't afford it. The check from the insurance company still hasn't shown up."

Shelby frowned at her. "We talked about this. I can lend you money until you get back on your feet."

She nodded, remembering Shelby's multiple offers to help after Naomi's shenanigans. As tempting as it sounded, borrowing money from Shelby made her uncomfortable. Call it leftover baggage from when Doug had "borrowed" money from her.

"I'll manage," she said. "What about dinner? We could get an early-bird special somewhere down here."

Shelby frowned but didn't argue. She stood, took Brianna's hand, and pulled her up. "I've got the perfect spot. Let's go."

They made the short walk to a steak place Brianna heard served the best twice-baked, bacon-wrapped potato in the city. She'd wanted to try it but heard it was impossible to get a reservation.

"What makes you think we'll be able to get in today?"

Shelby touched up her lipstick and smiled. "Let me work my magic."

Ten minutes later, the women were seated in a corner booth, champagne flutes filled with sparkling wine in front of them.

Shelby lifted her glass. "A toast to you and your new job!"

"And to the death of Prince Charming!"

Shelby sputtered, drops of wine dripping from her mouth. "So, I guess you don't want to hear about the guy who was admiring you the night you won the jackpot."

"Why did you wait an entire week to tell me?" Brianna asked. She knew it didn't matter. She'd sworn off men, but it would have been nice to know. "Details, please."

Brianna watched Shelby settle back into the cushions and take a sip of wine.

"You've had more important things to deal with than men, don't you think?"

"True. What did he say?"

"It's not what he *said* as much as . . ." Shelby paused when the server placed a charcuterie board in front of them. She waited until he was gone before she continued. "It's what he *did*."

Brianna thought about that evening as she helped herself to a piece of prosciutto and dipped it in the mustard sauce. Other than security intervening between the cat fight over the slot machine she had vacated, Brianna didn't recall any man doing anything.

"I have no idea what you're talking about."

She waited while Shelby chewed and swallowed the marinated mushroom she'd selected.

"You were in line cashing out. Some nimrod behind you looked like he was going to grab your butt. I started in that direction to intercept him, but this other guy was a couple steps ahead of me."

Brianna shook her head. "No one grabbed my butt that night. I would have remembered that."

Shelby plucked a piece of pepperoni off the board and popped it in her mouth. "The line moved before the asshat could get you."

Keeping her expression as neutral as possible, Brianna asked, "What's the difference between a nimrod and an asshat?"

Shelby arched her eyebrows and gave a one-fingered salute.

Grabbing her friend's hand, Brianna covered up the obscene gesture. "We're in a public place, you know."

Shaking off Brianna's hand, Shelby snagged a piece of Gruyère and waved it around.

"We're in Vegas. No one cares. Anyway, the point you're missing is that the guy was cute, and he wanted to get up the nerve to talk to you." Shelby took a bite of the cheese, then dropped it on her plate. "Ugh. I thought that was Parmesan. Nasty."

Brianna asked, "What did he look like? Did you get his name?"

A smile crept over Shelby's face, and she sat back and crossed her arms. "You're not looking for a guy any longer. Why would you want details like that?"

"Fine. Keep it to yourself." Brianna grabbed a fresh piece of Gruyère off the plate. She knew Shelby wouldn't be able to hold back. She popped the cheese in her mouth and waited.

"He wanted to know your name and if I thought he had a chance with you."

Déjà vu washed over her. That was what Doug had told her friend in Saint Thomas when they first met. She looked around the restaurant, scrutinizing the other diners. Doug couldn't be in Vegas, could he? Forcing the feeling aside, she assured herself that plenty of men—no, plenty of sharks— used that line.

Brianna picked up her champagne flute, determined not to let some random guy ruin her evening. "We need a toast." She raised her glass and waited for Shelby to raise hers. "To new beginnings and strong, independent women who don't need anyone but themselves—"

Shelby interrupted, "And a good friend!"

Nodding, Brianna continued, "To have a great time! Cheers!"

Their glasses clinked, and for the rest of the evening Brianna relaxed. She was ready for the next step in her journey. No one was going to stop her.

Chapter 14

Brianna stopped at the front door of Raeburn's property management office at precisely 8:59 the next morning. She caught her breath as she tugged at the lapel of her blazer. She smoothed down her favorite spaghetti-strap tank top with the pink French poodles. The shirt wasn't the most professional, but it made her feel good. Besides, Naomi had stolen her professional button-downs, which was also the reason she was wearing her black pleather pants. As long as no one looked too closely, they resembled a nice pair of slacks.

She hoped.

Closing her eyes, she took a deep breath. The hangover from last night's celebratory champagne with Shelby was down to a dull ache. It wasn't ideal, but she'd worked through worse. Besides, reporting to a woman would be a completely different experience than dealing with Alex.

Brianna pushed open the door and took in her surroundings. Five women and assorted children looked up at her when they heard her enter. Surprised that people were already waiting, she put a smile on her face and nodded at them as she made her way to the reception desk. She'd hoped to have time to settle in, but at least she wasn't late.

The woman at the reception desk didn't bother looking up. She slid a clipboard toward her and said, "Fill these out and have a seat. I'll call you back when it's your turn."

Brianna glanced down at the forms, which turned out to be application papers for an apartment. Wondering why the receptionist wasn't expecting her, she cleared her throat and said, "I'm not applying for an apartment. Today's my first day on the job. I'm looking for Gwen Martin."

The woman's head popped up, and a pair of sharp, amber eyes peered out, accentuated by thick charcoal eyeliner. Thin black eyebrows came together, forming a V on the woman's forehead as she surveyed Brianna from head to toe.

Brianna stepped back, unnerved by the judgement she saw in the woman's eyes. Apparently, the pink poodles and pleather pants were noticeable.

As the woman stood up and walked out from behind the desk, Brianna noticed her conservative black suit had a French flair to it, but it was the shoes that made her do a double take. She loved the four-inch designer heels, but they seemed out of place here.

"You're late. You were supposed to be here at eight."

Hoping to redeem herself, Brianna said, "Mr. Raeburn asked me to come at nine. I wanted to come by yesterday afternoon, but he said Gwen was out." She extended her hand. "I'm Brianna Thompson, by the way."

The woman stared at her hand. "I don't shake. Too many germs." She stood up and set out a sign that read, *Please fill out this paperwork and have a seat. Someone will be with you shortly*, then motioned to Brianna. "Follow me."

The woman didn't wait, and Brianna heard her heels click as she walked across the tile floor. Brianna turned to catch up but noticed a door ajar with Gwen Martin's name on it. Brianna frowned, wondering why they hadn't stopped. If she was late, she needed to apologize to Gwen as soon as possible.

Brianna peeked in the office, but instead of finding Gwen,

Brianna was transported to a Parisian café. Pictures of the Eiffel Tower adorned the walls, and a six-foot metal replica of the monument sat in the corner. A wrought-iron café table flanked by two chairs sat opposite the desk, which looked like the one she'd seen on display in a Marie Antoinette collection she'd seen years ago on a school field trip. An overwhelming floral scent hit her, and she sneezed.

"We're not meeting in my office," the woman said before pointing down the hall. "The conference room works better for the interviews."

"You're—" Brianna sneezed again, "you're Gwen Martin?"

"Of course I'm Gwen. Now, let's go. We have a schedule to keep."

Without another word, Gwen hurried down the hallway. Brianna sneezed again, then followed her silently. When they got to the conference room, Gwen walked to the head of the table and nodded at the stacks of paper on it.

"Mr. Raeburn clearly didn't give you the full rundown on things. Here's what you need to know for now: *I* run the office. You work for *me*. We are Mr. R's only two employees. The last receptionist left because she didn't like feeling sad after dealing with our clients. Her words, not mine. I'm swamped, and Mr. Raeburn thinks you walk on water. Sit down and we can get started."

So much for making a good first impression, Brianna thought as she sat down in one of the chairs.

"Has Mr. Raeburn told you what we do?" asked Gwen.

Brianna nodded, afraid to speak. She'd already messed up her first day by being nosy. She didn't want today to end like the time she'd temped for Sara Shaw. The attorney had needed a receptionist for a week, and Brianna was set to fill the position. She hadn't counted on Doug showing up or punching him in the face.

A shadow fell over her, and Brianna looked up. Gwen

stood over her, which was a feat. In heels, Gwen couldn't be more than five feet tall. Brianna realized she was as intimidated by this woman as she had been by Sara.

"Then you'll know we have a full schedule of interviews today. The interviews start at nine." Gwen glanced down at the silver bracelet watch on her left wrist. "It's 9:03. That's no way to treat these women. They've been through enough already."

Brianna started to apologize, but Gwen cut her off when she pushed a stack of files toward her.

"Read this. It's the application for our first interview. I review the files right before I meet the possible renters. Gives me a good sense of whether the person is telling the truth."

Brianna frowned. If they were late already, why would Gwen want her to read the file? Rather than question her, Brianna picked up the file folder and skimmed through its contents.

"People talk differently than they write, but you should be able to find the discrepancies in their intent." Gwen tapped the table with her fingers as if that would speed up Brianna's reading. "Each of Mr. Raeburn's applications has a background section. Read that and tell me what you think."

As she read through the woman's story, Brianna decided it reminded her a bit of herself. The applicant needed a place to stay for herself and her three children. Brianna gulped when she saw that none of the three dads provided financial support. The applicant noted the dads routinely asked her for money. None of them held down a job, but this mother of three currently had three jobs.

Brianna sat back to let the story sink in. How embarrassing to have to share this type of truth with a complete stranger. At least she and Doug didn't have children together. Although he did steal her money and leave her fighting for her professional career.

"Well?" asked Gwen. "What does this mean? Is this woman a good fit for our apartments?"

Knowing she needed to answer, Brianna chewed on the inside of her lip before she spoke. This applicant's life would be impacted by what she said. As could Brianna's new job.

"The part about having three jobs is easy enough to check. If that's the truth, then it makes sense she would work hard to get and keep this apartment."

She looked at Gwen for a response, but the woman stared at her, her face impassive. Brianna forged on.

"I understand having one child, but the other two are a mystery to me."

"Why is that?"

The question startled her. Was she being judgmental, or did she really have something to say about it? She used to let men walk all over her, which was why she was currently off men. It hadn't involved a child, but she'd let Doug take everything she had and had still been ready to give him more. Or she was until she saw how he'd acted around his ex-wife, Tasha. The way he treated his children baffled her. Blake and Libby were cute kids, but he pretended they didn't exist. Once she had seen his true feelings about children, she knew he would never be someone she wanted to start a family with.

"If my first experience with a man was that he rejected his child, I'd assume all men did that. That's not entirely true, but that would be what I would work from. I wouldn't want to do that to another child. Or myself, for that matter. It's hard enough to find someplace to live as a single person, let alone a single mother. I haven't experienced this level of rejection, but what I have felt hurts. I can't imagine what that hurt is like if it's targeted at a child."

Brianna knew that last sentence wasn't entirely true. She knew how upset Tasha had been when she learned Doug didn't bother to check on his kids when he was in town. Brianna might not have firsthand feelings about it, but seeing someone in pain because of the man they both loved left a mark.

"Do you have children?" Gwen asked.

The question caught her off guard. While this wasn't a job interview, it still felt weird to answer a personal question.

"No. I don't." Without thinking, Brianna continued. "I don't plan to, either."

Gwen's expression hardened, and Brianna knew she'd shared too much. Women had differing opinions on whether to have children. She knew better than to lob out her statement without expecting a reaction.

"Carl told me you were intuitive, but I'm surprised you identified this on your first interview."

Brianna's forehead crunched in confusion. "He said that about me?"

Gwen nodded at the application. "You're right. This woman likely has suffered a trauma that caused her low self-esteem. She lets these men take advantage of her to the point she has children with them and then is even further in debt. We can get her into an apartment, but that's not going to help if she keeps hooking up with people who take advantage of her. What do you think we should do?"

Brianna made a note that Gwen wasn't the person to ask for a pep talk before she answered the question.

"We could give her the apartment with the caveat that only she and her children can live there. That way, at least she can't have a boyfriend move in and take advantage of her good fortune." Brianna paused. Would things have been different if she'd had a rule in place about not dating clients when she and Doug got together? She might not have made such a mess of her life that way. Or she might have done exactly what she did and broken the rules anyway. "This woman might need a good reason to tell men no."

"For someone who worked for that scumbag Alex Dunderblatt, I didn't think you had it in you."

Brianna bit her tongue to keep from defending her former boss. Gwen was right, but it still hurt to know that she'd put up with working for Alex as long as she had. Instead, she nodded to Gwen.

"Should I go get our first interviewee?"

"Yes. Tell her to come on back," said Gwen. As Brianna headed to the door, Gwen called out, "How are you with kids? Someone is going to have to babysit while I talk to the mom."

Brianna swallowed her frustration. "I can figure it out," she said as she shuffled toward what was going to be a long day.

Gwen called her back. "Look, this isn't how I anticipated things turning out. If we had more time, I'd run you through some training, but we don't have the luxury of time today." Gwen took a deep breath and pointed to the door. "Talking to the kids is as important, if not more so, than interviewing the mothers. You need to figure out if the kids are safe and happy."

Brianna frowned. "I don't understand how that impacts the interview."

"These women have been through tough times, which means the kids have it worse. Most of them care for themselves and younger siblings after school. You can learn a lot about what's going on in the household by talking to the kids. Do you think you can do that?"

For someone as cold as Gwen appeared, she understood family dynamics. *This is why I wanted to work for a woman,* thought Brianna, who smiled and said, "Yes, I can."

Chapter 15

Forty-five minutes later, Brianna regretted her decision to wear the pleather pants. Not that she had many options, but the pants made it hard to sit on the floor. Plus, her pink poodle shirt was dirty from all the playing around.

She had been skeptical at first about Gwen's theory about kids, but Brianna understood Gwen's reasoning during the first interview.

When Gwen took the mother into the conference room, Brianna took the children to a connecting room with a glass window so that the mom and kids could see each other. Toys filled the room. Brianna was impressed by the variety of entertainment options and the fact that every child she interacted with found something they liked.

The children jumped at the chance to play. The siblings got along, were well-mannered, and were smart. Smarter than she was at that age. The seven-year-old read a book to the six-year-old while Brianna played a board game with the nine-year-old.

It didn't take much to find out from the boy, Wesley, that he wanted his own room and hoped his mother got the apartment.

"I love my sisters," he smiled up at her as he rolled the dice, "but boys need their space, you know?"

"Where do you live now?" Brianna asked, although she knew their last address was a women's shelter. Since Gwen wanted her to get intel on the family, that's what she planned to do.

The boy moved his playing piece around the board before he looked up at her. Brianna startled at the intensity of the look he gave her. He seemed to understand he was being interviewed, and he chose his words carefully.

"My baby sister's daddy is letting us stay in his basement until we find something else. Mom thinks this apartment is a good idea. It's close to our schools. We don't have to switch again, and we can still see Vanessa's daddy."

Brianna glanced over at Ashley, who was enjoying the story her older half sister, Vanessa, was reading before she took her turn.

"Have you changed schools a lot?"

"A couple times," the boy said. He watched as Brianna's playing piece landed on a square. "You owe me twenty-four dollars for rent."

Brianna counted out the play money and handed it to him. She watched as he sorted it neatly into stacks.

"You're pretty good. Play much?"

The boy nodded as he rolled again. "My daddy loves this game. I practice as much as I can. Next time I see him, I'm gonna win."

"When was the last time you saw him?"

Wesley's face fell. "Before he went to jail."

They played a few more rounds before their mother came into the room, followed by Gwen.

"Thank you for watching the kids, ma'am. Did they behave for you?"

Brianna stifled a grin. The woman knew the answer, as

Brianna had caught her throughout the interview checking to see what her children were doing.

"They were lovely. Wesley won the game, and your daughters read books."

"They have the book about the wizarding world, Mommy," Ashley called out. "The one with flying cars!"

The woman nodded as she said, "It's time to put things away. Our time here is up, and we need to let the next family in."

The children didn't argue and did as they were told. Brianna stood up and stretched as she watched the siblings work together, returning the playroom to its original state in a matter of minutes.

She followed Gwen and the family to the door, where Brianna's eyebrows raised when Gwen shook everyone's hands.

So much for germs, Brianna thought.

After the family left, Gwen led the way back to the conference room, whipping out hand sanitizer from her pocket.

"What did you think about the kids?" she asked Brianna as soon as the conference room door closed.

"Well-behaved. Super smart." Brianna thought about the differences between these kids and Doug's. "They seemed to like each other."

"Sound like good candidates for the apartment. The mother provided references from all her employers. I'll check them out, but she's qualified." Gwen pushed a file folder out for Brianna to see. "Read this and prepare yourself. I don't think this next interview is going to go as well."

As she read through the application, she noticed this woman was a widow with a twelve-year-old son. She immediately thought of Kevin and Rosemary. If the widow was anything like Kevin, things would be fine.

Brianna sighed in relief when they escorted the second family out of the office an hour later. Even though Brianna was in a separate room, she had heard the widow complaining about her situation. Her son, who hated reading and board games, had spent the entire time telling Brianna how mean his mother was.

"All she ever does is complain. My teachers won't talk to her, and I'm not allowed to go to my friends' houses. Nobody likes her."

She felt bad for the boy, but both she and Gwen agreed that this type of person would be a hassle to have in the unit. Nothing would be good enough for her. It made sense to eliminate her from contention.

The third, fourth, and fifth families fit the requirements for good tenants, although the fourth family consisted of a single woman who held down a job and didn't seem to be as needy as the others. The kids were a little wild in the fifth family, but otherwise Brianna thought things would work out well for them.

"How many open units are there?" Brianna asked as she closed the door after the last family left. "Other than the widow, I think these families would all be a good fit for what Mr. Raeburn is doing."

"We have three this round. There will be another five open next quarter." Gwen stacked the files she'd brought out of the conference room and tucked them into a briefcase. "Not that it's a good thing to label people, but I agree with your assessment of the widow. She would be tough to work with. And that last group of kids isn't going to work with the current tenants. Put them on the list for the next round, and send the widow a letter telling her she didn't make the cut."

Brianna nodded as her stomach growled. "Okay. Can I grab something to eat before that?" She glanced at her watch and noticed it was almost three o'clock. "I can be quick."

Gwen frowned. "I need you to cover the phones while you fill out your new hire paperwork," she said as she pushed a stack of papers toward Brianna. She slung the briefcase over her shoulder and crossed her arms over her chest.

Brianna felt a lecture coming on. She was right.

"Despite the way you dress and the fact that you were late," Gwen raised a disapproving eyebrow, "you can handle the job. I've got an appointment. I'll be back by five to show you how to lock up. Have your paperwork completed and bring your lunch tomorrow."

Brianna's stomach rumbled, but she remained silent as Gwen left the conference room. She waited until the sound of Gwen's heels was further down the hallway before she got up and went to the door. Brianna saw her new boss go into her office and come right back out. She recognized a look of irritation on Gwen's face as she pointed toward the reception area.

"Phones are that way. Take your paperwork out there."

Brianna walked down the hallway and reached the reception area in time to see the front door close. So much for working with someone who valued her work. Gwen might be as difficult as Alex after all.

Chapter 16

Doug swirled the red wine in his glass and looked at his watch. Not only was his contact late for their meeting, this stupid replica of a sidewalk café in the middle of a Las Vegas casino didn't serve his preferred Scotch. He grimaced as he sipped the wine and shook his head. The guy who told him about the job had warned him.

"She plays by her own rules."

Considering how much he needed the money, he thought he could handle it. It damn well better be worth it, especially to put up with croissants and foie gras.

The server came over, and Doug ordered another glass of wine.

"Would you like to order food with that?"

"Still waiting." Doug read into the server's question. He hadn't been stood up and he wasn't drunk. Yet. "She'll be here. Women are always late, you know?"

The man pursed his lips and walked away. Doug didn't know what it was, but the server sure as hell was uptight. Who cared if he drank his lunch? If his contact didn't show up, he'd have a good buzz going for his afternoon cruise of the casinos. One of these days, he was bound to run into China again.

"Excuse me."

A woman wearing all black stood next to the table. Her bright-red lipstick stood out against her pale face.

He rolled his eyes. "I told the other guy I didn't want to order. Buzz off."

The woman's thin black eyebrows clamped together in a V, making her look like one of the original Klingons. She held her black leather purse with both hands in front of her and stood up straight as an arrow. He decided she looked more like Wednesday Addams than a Klingon.

"You're Doug, I presume. Rodney warned me you were an ass."

Doug covered his surprise by leaning back on the wrought-iron patio chair. He stared back at the woman. As much as he needed the job, he didn't want to let this chick know it. From experience, he knew the best way to deal with a bully was to be a bully. He got to work.

She had likely spent a small fortune on her hair and face, but it did nothing for him. The suit she wore disguised her body. He preferred women in dresses, but then he noticed her four-inch black stilettos. The Valentinos aroused him, making it impossible to stand up if he wanted to.

Great! he thought. *A contact with fashion sense. And an attitude.*

He squirmed in his seat, adjusting his jeans to get more comfortable before he cleared his throat. "You'd be Gwen. Rodney told me you were a piece of work." Her eyebrows shot up, and he allowed himself a smirk. Now that she knew the score, the negotiations could begin. "Have a seat."

She looked down at him, which was a challenge even though she was standing in heels. The woman couldn't have been much taller than his daughter, who was seven. No, wait, maybe Libby was eight. He banished the thought from his head. If he was going to get this job, he needed to focus.

Gwen lowered her chin and narrowed her eyes, as if she were deciding whether to continue the game. Doug held his breath. He might have overplayed his cards, but he needed to make sure she knew what he was capable of. That was the only way people like him got hired.

As soon as she pulled out the chair, he let out his breath. He didn't say anything while she flagged down a server and placed her order. Doug saw her glance at his wine, and he detected an air of disapproval. He let it go. He'd play nice until he knew exactly what the job was and what he could make. If it wasn't to his liking, he was out of here.

The server left, and Gwen folded her hands on the table in front of her. "Are you capable of helping me?" she asked.

"Direct and to the point. That's how I like my women."

She stared back at him. "That's not an answer."

"You haven't told me what you need."

"Rodney didn't explain?"

Doug shook his head and finished his wine. He waited for her to continue, but she just sat there. She gazed around the café and nodded at people as they passed. The server came by with Doug's third glass of wine and assured Gwen her food would be out soon. Gwen remained silent.

After a few more minutes, Doug decided he didn't like Gwen much. She was pushy, condescending, and self-centered. He shook his head. The problem was he didn't have the luxury of liking this woman. He needed the job.

He cleared his throat to ask Gwen the details when she gave him a quick shake of her head. Their order appeared then. The server put down a salad and a glass of sparking water with lemon before giving a quick nod and leaving them alone.

Gwen didn't touch either the food or drink. Instead, she launched into an explanation of what she wanted from Doug. The work was straightforward, though time-consuming and backbreaking. His sole responsibility was to move all the furnishings out of apartments and into a storage unit without being seen. Then he had to replace them with similar but cheaper versions he would find in a second storage unit.

"You'll deal with me most of the time, though my employer hired a receptionist who you may interact with from time to time. She doesn't know what's happening, nor does she ever need to be in on things."

"Is your employer in on it?" The job sounded tamer than the ones Rodney usually recommended. The best Doug could tell, she was scamming her boss, but the scam was too big for her to pull off alone. He got his answer when she smiled.

"That's information you don't need at this time."

"What's in it for me?"

Gwen named an amount that would facilitate Doug's Scotch-drinking and gambling habits while he was in town, and he nodded his approval.

"Fine. I'll be in touch."

Without further explanation, she picked up her fork and ate her salad. Her demeanor both confused and aroused him again. He remained in his seat and sipped his wine. The alcohol burned Doug's throat as he watched her eat one bite of lettuce at a time. She was messing with him.

Doug recognized the similarities between her actions and his own. Partially accommodate a person, but not all the way. Make them comfortable enough that they can't complain, but not comfortable enough that they get their bearings. He had done this all the time to his ex-wife, at least until she had married Greg. For whatever reason, that asshole gave her the power to ignore him. Annoying that it had to be one of his friends who gave her a backbone, but *c'est la vie*.

Damn it. This French place is rubbing off on me.

Doug slammed back the rest of his wine and stood up. He wobbled more than he would have liked, but he didn't care. This woman needed him, and now he knew about her business. If she wanted to judge him, he could cause a boatload of problems for her. And she didn't want that. She had too much at stake. And he, as usual, had nothing to lose.

"Thanks for the drinks," he said.

Gwen's nostrils flared, and he knew he'd hit the mark. The hatred in her eyes confirmed she knew the score, and he relaxed as he stumbled out of the café.

Chapter 17

The reporter cracked her knuckles. Cynthia hadn't heard from Sara or Gwen since she'd sent them emails the prior week, and her editor wanted an update. She wasn't surprised Sara hadn't responded, but she was confused by Gwen's silence. Everyone liked positive free press, and she didn't know why the company wouldn't be excited to be written up.

If an email didn't work, maybe a phone call would. She shuffled through the papers on her desk. Somewhere, mixed in with the flyers for apartments for rent and houses for sale, was the press release with Gwen's contact information. Cynthia hadn't made any more progress on what to do with her living situation other than collect paper. She couldn't keep putting it off forever, but before she had time to dwell on it, she found the press release.

She dialed Gwen's phone number and was greeted by, "Good afternoon. Raeburn Property Management."

"Yes, my name is Cynthia Anderson. I'm a reporter for *The Gazette*. We received a press release on the apartments your company is making available to women in need. I was wondering if I could speak to Gwen Martin about the project."

Cynthia frowned at the long pause that followed her question. She started to ask again when the voice finally responded.

"Gwen is out right now. I can leave a message for her. You said Cynthia Anderson with *The Gazette*? That's in Glen Valley, right?"

The fact that the receptionist knew Glen Valley threw Cynthia for a moment. No one knew about the little town. Who was she talking to?

"Yes, that's correct. Let me give you my number." She rattled it off along with her email address. "Can you tell me what Gwen's title is? I'd like to include that in my notes."

"She's the property manager. She's the one who put out the press releases. I'll be sure she gets your message. Have a good day."

"Wait," Cynthia called out. The last thing she wanted to do was leave another message that might not get returned. Her investigative instincts kicked in and Cynthia said, "I wanted to thank you. I don't always get helpful people on the line. Would you mind giving me your name? That way, if I have more questions, I can give you a call back."

The line went quiet again, and Cynthia's spider sense buzzed. There was a connection. If the receptionist had a name, it wouldn't take long to figure it out.

"I'm the receptionist here. Anytime you call, I'll answer the phone." Cynthia heard a man speaking in the background, and the receptionist said, "Can you hold a moment?"

New-age music met her ear before she could respond, and Cynthia sat back in her chair. Why didn't the woman just give her name? She glanced at the press release. Raeburn Property Management was located in Las Vegas. It seemed odd the receptionist had heard of *The Gazette*. If she didn't already have a story, Cynthia might use this as a distraction to do some investigating. It was nice to make sure her skills didn't get rusty.

The music ended abruptly, and a man said, "Hello. This is Carl Raeburn. I understand you're interested in our housing project. How can I help you?"

Cynthia's eyes widened. She couldn't believe her luck. Much better to talk to the owner of the company than the property manager. She introduced herself and explained the purpose of her call. That was all it took for Raeburn to spend the next hour telling her about the project and answering all her questions about how the Miller Agency had partnered with them to make housing affordable for women and children in need.

When Raeburn encouraged her to call Sara, Cynthia let him know she'd already reached out.

"Wonderful. Let me know if you have any trouble getting hold of her. I'd be happy to ask either her or Jared to call you. Ms. Shaw has been a rock as we have ramped up our outreach. Without her knowledge and legal skill, the Women's Shelter and Support Agency wouldn't have made it this far."

"Thank you for the information. I'll keep that in mind, Mr. Raeburn. You wouldn't believe the number of people who put out press releases then don't want to talk about what they're doing." Cynthia couldn't help adding, "Your receptionist helped as well. Do you mind if I ask where you found her? We're looking for someone new at our office."

She recognized the sound of pride in Raeburn's voice when he said, "Brianna is our latest hire. I found her myself, as a matter of fact. She worked with one of our partners."

Cynthia jotted down the name on her notepad before asking, "What's her last name? I'd like to include everyone in the office in the article."

"Thompson. It's actually her first day on the job, but I'm glad to have her on board. We run a tight ship around here. It's just the three of us—Gwen, Brianna, and me."

Getting back to conversation, Cynthia said, "Well, whatever role Brianna has, I appreciate her time. And yours. If I have any follow-up questions, can I give you a call?"

"Absolutely. Be sure to let me know when the story is published. It's good to get the word out on what we're doing."

They said their goodbyes and, after the call ended, Cynthia straightened up the notes she'd made. She slid them into a file folder, where they would wait until Sara returned her call, and leaned back in her chair. Usually phone interviews were enough, but something told her this story needed an onsite visit. Raeburn's passion came through over the phone, but a firsthand view of the Women's Shelter and Support Agency might give the story an extra kick.

Unfortunately the newspaper didn't have the budget for a trip, and Cynthia couldn't afford to pay for it herself. All her spare money needed to go into her savings for when she found somewhere to live. She rubbed the back of her neck, hoping Sara would come through. It wouldn't be as good as a face-to-face meeting, but it might be all she had.

Speaking of which, the name Brianna Thompson didn't leave her with much. Cynthia was pretty good with names, and the fact that she couldn't place where she'd heard it before irked her. There were no Thompsons in Glen Valley, and she didn't know anyone in Las Vegas. Maybe she had heard it in passing. It was a common enough name.

With a sigh, she put the file folder in her desk drawer. Cynthia refused to draft a story without all the research in front of her. Until she heard back from Sara, she needed to move on to other stories.

Cynthia grabbed the papers closest to her and grimaced. Of course she would pick up Helene's draft for choosing a wedding dress. Cynthia grabbed her red pen and started marking.

Chapter 18

The following week at work kept Brianna busy. When Gwen had returned from her appointment on Brianna's first day, she was in a worse mood than when she'd left. She spat out directions to Brianna and was condescending when Brianna didn't understand things the first time.

"I can't believe this is what I have to work with," Gwen said more than once.

Brianna considered telling her supervisor that if she took the time to actually explain what she wanted, it might help, but she knew that would make things worse. Brianna didn't think anyone could be worse than Alex, but she gritted her teeth and did her best.

Despite the rude comments, Gwen let Brianna handle everything about the office. Raeburn was right—one person couldn't do this job alone. Someone was always dropping into the office or calling about available apartments. It broke Brianna's heart to see the kids' faces when she told their moms there was a waiting list. She got in the habit of sending a toy or book home with each of the kids, even though she knew that didn't change the fact that they were heading back to the shelter—or worse, an abusive situation.

When she wasn't talking to families, Brianna ordered furnishings for the apartments and houses. She took a crash course in bookkeeping and took over the day-to-day finances. Brianna even ran background checks for the new tenants.

She was swamped and didn't have much time or energy to do any practice or review for her real estate licensing test. It was great that she had a better-paying job in a friendlier environment, although that was debatable depending on Gwen's mood. But she still wanted her license back and wasn't making as much progress as she had hoped.

Every day, Brianna studied for the test during her lunch hour, but the fifteen minutes she got to scarf down the sandwich she'd brought from home didn't offer a lot of time, and she frequently got interrupted by phone calls or urgent requests from Gwen. Gwen's three-hour lunches and afternoons out of the office didn't help matters.

On the bright side, Brianna got to know Carl Raeburn. He always stopped at her desk when he arrived in the office, chatting to see how things were going. He even brought her lunch one day.

"I hope you don't mind." He held out a bag of food, and her stomach growled when the warm smell of fresh cooking hit her nose. "Here's something from my favorite café. You deserve it for the hard work you've been putting in."

"That's kind of you." Brianna took the bag and opened it. All her senses piqued in anticipation of the hearty soup and enormous sandwich, which looked to be made with artisan bread. "Thank you."

"Tell me how things are going."

Her mouth watered as she closed the bag and set it on the desk. As appetizing as the food was, she needed to answer Raeburn's questions first, and she kept her concerns about Gwen to herself. She knew not to make waves. Instead, Brianna got Raeburn up to speed on the growing list of women wanting apartments and the progress on several properties before she handed him the stack of phone messages she'd taken.

"You get a lot of requests for interviews," she said as she handed over messages from five different newspapers. "Do you take them all?"

He flicked through the messages and shook his head. "I do a few. It helps to get the word out, but there are journalists who are looking for the wrong angle." Brianna cringed when he tossed the messages in the trash. "It's okay. I've dealt with all those people before. They're looking to help themselves, not the women and children who need our help. I can afford to be selective. Have you heard anything back from that reporter at *The Gazette*? I'm wondering if Sara got back to her."

Hearing the name Sara silenced Brianna's stomach mid-growl. This couldn't be the same Sara Shaw she knew. But why else would Cynthia from *The Gazette* reach out? Brianna wanted to slap her forehead for not seeing the connection before. She took a few deep breaths as she convinced herself it didn't matter anyway. Raeburn liked her work. He wouldn't care if she knew the other women. And he didn't seem like the type of person who would judge her for her past behaviors.

Brianna's stomach recovered before her emotions and growled again, making Raeburn laugh.

"I've talked long enough. Eat your lunch. I'll be in my office for a bit. Let me know if you have any questions." He walked down the hall, then turned back, "Oh, and if Gwen's not back by five, you're free to leave. You've put in some long hours. I don't want to burn you out."

As soon as she heard his door click shut, Brianna reached for the bag of food, although with less enthusiasm now that she knew what her near future held.

Steam poured off the baked potato soup when she unsealed the container, and she let it cool while she tried the turkey club sandwich. As she chewed the decadent sandwich complete with cranberry spread and bacon, she memorized the name of the deli from the delivery bag. She'd be a frequent patron from here on out. Plus, it might be a nice to have the deli deliver a welcome basket to each of the new renters. She jotted down the suggestion to bring up with Gwen or Raeburn.

With a sigh, Brianna chastised herself for stalling. She needed to confirm her suspicions about Sara and decide how she would deal with it if she came face-to-face with her.

She savored the soup as she turned to her computer and did some online sleuthing. She knew Raeburn's partner, Jared, fixed up the apartments to be rented. She'd even traded emails with him. But what she hadn't known was that he was Jared Hughes of the Miller Agency, the same man she'd met while she was temping in Sara's office. From there, it didn't take long to discover Sara now worked for the Miller Agency as inside counsel.

All that was left to do was decide if she should be worried or not. At some point, she and Sara were bound to talk to each other. Maybe she should call Sara and get the awkwardness out of the way sooner than later.

The front door opened before she could make a decision, and Gwen's high heels clicked on the tile. Brianna rushed to put the remains of her lunch back in the bag but wasn't fast enough.

"I thought I was clear about no eating at the desk." Gwen frowned as she shifted her shopping bag from one arm to the other. Brianna didn't know if the woman did it intentionally or not, but Gwen seemed to flaunt her lunchtime purchases. Gwen sniffed the air and looked at the bag on Brianna's desk. "Where did you get that? I told you not to leave your desk while I'm gone."

"Mr. Raeburn brought it for me."

Gwen's demeanor changed at the mention of her boss's name. She smoothed out her ever-present black attire and looked toward his office. "Why didn't you tell me he was here? That *is* your job, you know."

Gwen hurried down the hallway. Brianna heard a door open and the unmistakable sound of bags hitting the floor. The door closed, then footsteps sounded, followed by a knock on a door.

"Mr. Raeburn, I'm back. Can I have a moment?"

Brianna didn't hear his response, but a second door opened and closed.

Relieved to have Gwen occupied, she tidied up her desk and ran her leftover lunch to the break room refrigerator before sitting down to work on accounts payable. Brianna picked up the invoices for the latest apartment that was renovated: 6483 Birch. Raeburn furnished his units with top-of-the-line appliances and accessories, which meant each invoice had hundreds of purchase orders to match up. She sorted through the stack and matched them up to the documents she'd gotten from Gwen. Things went smoothly until she got to three invoices from a plumbing supply company but no packing slips that matched up.

She frowned. The same thing had happened earlier in the week with the same vendor. When she'd bought it to Gwen's attention, the woman had shrugged.

"That company doesn't include packing slips. Don't worry about it. Pay the bills like I told you and shred the rest. We don't need backup for paid items, and I don't like a lot of clutter around the office."

Brianna added up the discrepancies and shook her head. She refused to shred anything until she talked to Gwen. It looked like this vendor was charging them for items they had never delivered. If she paid the bills now, she'd never be able to get the money back. And she didn't want to be on the hook for thousands of dollars.

Making a neat stack of the invoices in question, Brianna set them aside and reached for the bank statement to reconcile. Before she could start, she heard a door open and someone stomping down the hall. Brianna expected Gwen to appear in the reception area. Usually, after Gwen talked with Raeburn, Brianna got more work. This time, no one showed up in the lobby. A door slammed, letting Brianna know now was not a good time to talk to her boss. She'd have to wait to pay the bill.

Chapter 19

The key to her apartment stuck in the lock. Brianna's shoulders fell. She didn't have the energy to deal with the finicky lock tonight—not after the long, arduous day she'd had. Raeburn had told her she could leave at five, but Gwen gave her another stack of tenant applications to review and told her not to leave until she'd made notes on each one. Of course, Gwen left promptly at five after snatching the plumbing invoices off Brianna's desk.

"This company isn't going to work with us anymore if you don't pay them."

Brianna had held her ground. "There's no documentation of what they sold us."

"I told you before—they don't issue packing slips. I'll take care of this myself." Gwen had shoved the papers in her bag and pointed at the receipts on Brianna's desk. "And shred those stupid receipts. We don't need a bunch of paper mucking up the office."

Brianna had stuck around the office until nine thirty, when the words on the applications started to blur. The applications and receipts weighed down her briefcase. She'd brought them home, hoping she could work on them after dinner.

But she'd forgotten about the door lock.

She leaned her head against the door and counted to ten before she pulled on the key. Without warning, it slid out, and she stepped backward to catch herself. The briefcase pulled at her side, and her heel caught on the hallway carpet, twisting her ankle in the process.

"Damn it," she mumbled as pain throbbed in her foot.

She checked the door handle, but it was still locked.

Sinking to the hallway floor, she held back tears. The lock needed to be fixed, but she had forgotten to call the super during business hours. It was too late now. Brianna looked around, but no one else was in the hall. Not that she knew anyone. Other than Kevin in 8C.

Brianna considered hobbling up to Kevin's apartment. She imagined what he would do when he looked through the peephole of his door and saw her standing there. Part of her wanted to believe he would be fine with her dropping by this late. It's not like she was there for a social visit. Maybe he had tools she could use to open the door.

Shaking her head, Brianna admitted she didn't know how to open a door with anything other than a key. She grabbed the deli bag with her leftover lunch and dug out the sandwich. Maybe she'd have a better idea what to do after eating something.

The remaining sandwich tasted as good as the half she'd eaten earlier. She gobbled it down, then looked longingly at the soup container. Cold soup didn't sound appetizing. She stuffed it back in the bag before standing up. Testing her injured foot, Brianna relaxed when the pain was less than before.

Hoping her luck would hold, Brianna took a deep breath as she inserted the key again. She twisted her wrist back and forth, slowly and methodically. The process took a few minutes, but she smiled when she heard the lock release. Opening the door, she dropped her briefcase on the floor.

Papers cascaded out, but she made a beeline to the kitchen to heat up the rest of her dinner. She'd pick up the mess later.

She made short work of the soup and got an ice pack for her ankle before deciding to give up on work. If she set her alarm clock for an hour earlier than usual, she'd have time to finish the applications in the morning. Brianna cleaned up the kitchen, turned off the lights, and limped toward her bedroom when she heard a knock at her door.

Brianna ignored it. She was exhausted and had another long day ahead of her tomorrow. But whoever it was kept knocking. Then she recognized Kevin's voice as he called out, "Brianna, if you're there, answer the door. It's an emergency."

Without giving it another thought, Brianna rushed to the door and flung it open.

Kevin stood in front of her, an expression of panic on his face that improved slightly when he saw her.

"I'm sorry to bother you this late, but I don't have a lot of options."

That's when Brianna noticed a young girl standing next to him and holding a box. She resembled Kevin, but the guarded look in the girl's eyes reminded Brianna of the kids from the office. This girl knew pain. This must be Kevin's daughter, Rosemary.

Pulling her eyes off the girl, Brianna looked at Kevin and said, "It's okay. I just got home from work. What can I do?"

Kevin glanced at his daughter before he said, "I know this is asking a lot. You don't know me very well, but a friend of mine needs help and I can't take Rosemary. I don't have anyone else to call. Could she stay with you until I get back? It may be a while. She brought a puzzle to keep her busy."

Brianna looked at Rosemary again and caught the girl's eyes darting to the floor. She bit her lip. The last thing she wanted to do was babysit, but Kevin had helped her out before. This was the least she could do.

"Okay. But shouldn't we stay at your apartment? That

would be more familiar to her." She nodded over her shoulder. "Besides, I don't have furniture. And doesn't she have school tomorrow?"

The expression on Kevin's face told her she was protesting too much. She couldn't help it. She didn't know if she had the energy to deal with this tonight.

"Tomorrow is a teacher in-service day, and you don't need furniture. She can do the puzzle on the floor and take a nap in the beanbag if she gets tired." His phone buzzed and he looked at it. "Is it okay? If not, tell me, but I have to go."

Knowing she'd regret it before the night was over, Brianna put out her hand. "Give me your phone. I'll put my number in. Keep me posted on when you'll be back."

Kevin handed over the phone. Brianna watched Kevin say goodbye to his daughter out of the corner of her eye, then gave him his phone and opened the door wide.

"Come on in. Let's get comfy!"

The girl shuffled in and sat down in the center of the almost-empty living room. She opened the box and dumped out the puzzle, the tiny pieces clattering when they hit the floor.

Brianna turned back to Kevin and nodded. "Looks like we're good here."

Brianna's heart rate picked up when Kevin stepped forward with his arms out. Before he could hug her, Brianna saw his eyes dart to where Rosemary sat, and Kevin stopped. As much as she wanted the hug, she understood why he shouldn't. It was for the best.

She heard Kevin's phone buzz again, and she waved him back. "You better get going. Your friend needs you."

Kevin gave a quick nod. She thought he was going to say something, but instead, he turned and headed down the stairs. Brianna closed the door to the sound of him taking the steps two at a time.

Brianna leaned back against the door and watched Rosemary work. The girl's fingers flew through the pieces, separating them by color. When she found the straight edges for the outside border, Rosemary lined them up. When she got several pieces in a row that went together, she connected them, then went back to the separating process. Rosemary worked fast. If she kept it up, she'd be finished long before her father returned.

Brianna cleared her throat. It might be a good idea to slow down the progress. "Would you like a glass of water? Sorry, I don't have anything else. I wasn't expecting company tonight."

Without looking up, Rosemary said, "No, thank you," and continued.

Not sure what else to do, Brianna walked into the living room and sat down on the floor. She picked up the puzzle box, which advertised the jigsaw had one thousand pieces and was recommended for adults looking for a challenging experience. Rosemary didn't seem challenged at all. The border of one side was almost complete, and she'd started putting together the bottom edge.

"Do you want any help?"

Rosemary shook her head. "No. I can do it myself."

Certain that the girl was capable of doing it herself, Brianna asked, "Have you done this one before?"

Again, the girl shook her head.

So much for small talk, thought Brianna. *I shouldn't be surprised. I didn't like talking to adults when I was her age, either.*

Brianna tried again. "How did you get so good at this?"

This time Rosemary stopped what she was doing and stared at Brianna.

Brianna shivered. The girl's ice-blue eyes looked like her father's, but where Kevin's were warm and inviting, Rosemary's felt cold and angry.

"Why do you ask so many questions?"

The accusation caught Brianna off guard, and she

blinked, breaking eye contact. Brianna looked down and noticed a piece that would fit into the bottom border. She picked it up and snapped it into place before she answered. "I wanted to make you comfortable." She swallowed before she looked back up.

Rosemary stared at the puzzle piece Brianna placed before she picked up another piece and connected it. "You can stop. I don't want your sympathy. My dad and I are fine." Without looking up, Rosemary added, "Your plant needs watered."

Brianna looked over at Philomena and saw Rosemary was right. The philodendron's leaves drooped, and a few had fallen off. She'd been so busy with her new job she'd forgotten to water it.

She took care of her plant, then settled back down on the floor next to Rosemary. The two of them worked in silence. Every few minutes, Brianna felt Rosemary's eyes on her, but she didn't engage the girl. Kevin had told her Rosemary preferred to be alone. She shouldn't have pried. It had to be tough growing up without a mom.

Plus, the girl was in a stranger's apartment, and it was late. Maybe Rosemary was tired and wanted to go to bed?

That's where Brianna wanted to be right now. The day's events had exhausted her, and she wasn't thinking clearly.

Brianna stifled a yawn when Rosemary asked, "Are you going to tell my dad?"

"Tell him what?"

"That I was rude to you?"

Brianna dropped the puzzle piece she was holding and looked up at Rosemary. The girl's eyes no longer appeared angry. She looked scared.

Picking up the piece again, Brianna set it in place. "No. You saved my plant. I owe you." She studied the girl, who held her gaze. Brianna's curiosity won out. "But why were you rude?"

Rosemary shrugged. "I like things the way they are. Dad and me. The therapist says my dad will date again, but I don't think so. He misses my mom too much."

Brianna waited a few seconds to make sure she could speak without her voice cracking. She wondered if Kevin knew about his daughter's feelings.

"Well, I'm just helping your dad out. Not dating him. Besides, I've given up on men. We're all safe."

The girl studied her face and nodded. "I believe you," Rosemary said before she asked sheepishly, "Can I have your plant? Dad won't let me have a dog, but he might agree to a plant."

Brianna shook her head. "Sorry. Philomena was a gift." She avoided mentioning it was from her mother but suggested, "You could always get your own from the store."

Rosemary nodded and went back to work. She placed a few pieces together before she pointed to the door. "Your papers fell out of your bag."

Brianna stood up and gathered them up. She had a neat pile when she heard Rosemary's voice at her side. The girl had followed her to look at the papers.

"What is all that stuff?" Rosemary picked up a sheet and studied it.

"It's a puzzle from my office."

Rosemary's head popped up. "This isn't a puzzle. It's a bunch of paper."

"Well, technically, you're right. But the numbers on each of those papers are supposed to have receipts that add up to the total amount. They don't. I have to figure out why."

The girl's eyes got wide. "Are you a forensic accountant?"

Brianna shoved the receipts back into her briefcase. "No, I'm not. I'm not even sure what that means."

The expression on Rosemary's face made Brianna want to laugh, but she didn't want to damage the progress they'd made.

"It's not a common career," said Rosemary, and Brianna listened as the girl explained what the forensic accountant had shared with her class on Career Day.

Chapter 20

"He dropped her off and expected you to babysit?" Shelby's voice was muffled over the phone, but her tone was unmistakable. Shelby didn't approve. "That's assuming a lot, if you ask me."

Brianna agreed, but the night had ended well. Kevin had returned shortly before eleven, only a few minutes after Rosemary had finished the puzzle and her explanation on forensic accounting. Brianna hadn't even had time to worry about what to do next.

"He came to my rescue with the coffeepot and plates and stuff. It was the least I could do. I was home anyway."

"Fine. But be careful. Don't make it a habit or people will take advantage of you."

Brianna glanced at the work stacked up on her desk and decided now was not the time to tell Shelby how she was doing almost all the work in Raeburn's office. Since she'd started, Gwen had spent more and more time out of the office. It felt like Brianna was back to the girl Friday routine.

"I switched jobs. Don't you think that's a step in the right direction?"

Casino noises made it impossible to hear Shelby's

response. Brianna waited for the background noise to quiet before she asked, "What did you say?"

"Have you made any progress on your real estate license?"

Brianna didn't want to admit she'd given up trying to study. One day, when Gwen had walked out of the office on one of her long lunches, she had noticed what Brianna was doing.

"What in the world do you think you're doing? I don't pay you to mess around online all afternoon. Do you think those invoices are going to pay themselves?" Gwen had taken the opportunity to flaunt her new designer clothing while she lectured. "Mr. Raeburn might have hired you, but if I let him know you're not doing your job, you can go straight back to Alex Dunderblatt's office."

"Some progress," Brianna lied to Shelby. "It's hard to find the time. I'm exhausted when I get home at night."

"And let's not forget that you're babysitting for free for a man you hardly know."

Brianna knew Shelby meant well. Rather than argue, she changed the subject.

"How's your work going? Anything interesting?"

"Other than the floor manager whose girlfriend gets preferential treatment? She got the primo shift for the third week in a row. I'm tired of getting stuck with the bad shifts because I won't sleep with my boss."

Brianna tuned out Shelby's rant. She'd heard it several times, and it was getting worse. Shelby should file a complaint, although Brianna understood why she didn't. It was the same as when she had worked for Alex. Brianna didn't want to rock the boat. She had put up with a lot of things that didn't seem right to get a paycheck. Thankfully, she was past that now. Raeburn's office wasn't perfect, but it was a huge step in the right direction.

"Are you listening to anything I've said?"

The question startled Brianna, but she'd heard enough to know how to answer.

"The floor manager sucks, and his girlfriend sucks more. But you can't file a report because that makes you look like a complainer, and complainers don't get promoted."

She was rewarded with a low whistle.

"Oh. You *were* listening." A muffled voice called Shelby's name. "I've got to go. Get to work on the real estate license. I might need a realtor soon."

The line went dead before Brianna could ask her friend what she was talking about. She knew Shelby had a house fund, but she didn't know how much was in it. The phone rang before she could give it another thought.

"Raeburn Property Management. How can I help you?"

"Brianna?"

The hairs on her neck stood up. Who would be calling for her?

"Yes. This is Brianna."

"Oh, good. This is Cynthia Anderson from *The Gazette*. How are you this afternoon?"

Unsure why it mattered, Brianna forced herself to respond. "Fine, thank you. Mr. Raeburn isn't in this afternoon. I can leave him a message if you'd like."

"No, actually, I was calling for you."

Brianna shivered even though the office was warm. "What can I do for you?"

"For starters, you can tell me why your name is familiar."

Brianna didn't want to tell Cynthia who she was. People in Glen Valley didn't like her. What if Cynthia told Sara and Sara told Raeburn? Would he keep her on staff?

"It's a pretty common name. You could have heard it anywhere."

The minute she said it, Brianna felt an urge to come clean. Who was she kidding? Cynthia was bound to find out anyway.

Brianna might as well be the one who told her. It might give her some control over the situation.

"I temped at Smith Rogers Shaw for a day a few months ago."

Silence followed her announcement. Brianna gave Cynthia a full minute to make the connection. Everyone in Glen Valley thought Brianna had ruined Doug's marriage. She suspected everyone knew about the left hook she had taken him down with as well as the altercation with Sara. Gossip ran wild in small towns, especially when a major contributor like Helene Shaw happened to be the lawyer's mother.

Cynthia finally said, "Oh. You're China."

Brianna shook her head. The last thing she wanted was her past hijinks to affect her job or the story that Cynthia was doing on Raeburn. His project was too important to be derailed.

"My name is Brianna. China was Doug's nickname for me."

"Have you told Sara?"

Frustration set in, and Brianna palmed her forehead. "No. I didn't realize Sara and Jared worked with Mr. Raeburn until you called. It's not like I can call Sara out of the blue and tell her."

The second she uttered the words, Brianna regretted it. If Cynthia hadn't already come up with the idea on her own, Brianna had just given her the suggestion that could complicate things even more. She didn't know much about the history between Cynthia and Sara, but she did know they didn't get along. Brianna imagined this juicy bit of information was too much for the reporter to keep to herself.

"I have a call in to Sara."

Cynthia's statement didn't surprise her. She wouldn't be doing her job if she didn't contact everyone involved in the project.

"I could mention that you and I spoke," Cynthia continued. "Put in a good word for you. And tell her how much Mr. Raeburn likes working with you as well."

Hope filled Brianna. If she had enough people on her side, Sara wouldn't make a big deal of the fact that she was working here. She didn't know how much pull Sara had with Raeburn, but she did know he valued her work ethic. Maybe it wouldn't matter what baggage she carried. He'd want her to stay.

Before she could decide what to tell Cynthia, the front door flew open, and Gwen's perfume wafted in. Brianna sneezed as she panicked. Rather than explain this conversation to her boss, she rushed to end the call with Cynthia.

"Thanks for the offer. I'll think about it. I've got to go."

She hung up the phone before Cynthia could say anything. She turned to her computer and began to check email as Gwen walked up and stood in front of her desk.

"Who was that?" Gwen nodded at the phone, the Louis Vuitton and Manolo Blahnik shopping bags rubbing against her usual black attire. "That sounded like a personal call. Personal calls aren't allowed. We've been over this."

Not for the first time, Brianna wondered how Gwen afforded such expensive shoes before she focused on answering the question. Brianna made a nice salary, but she was barely getting by. She still needed to replace the furniture Naomi had stolen.

"It was a reporter calling about the press releases you sent out."

The vein in Gwen's smooth forehead throbbed. "Why didn't you give me the call, then? I'm right here."

Brianna didn't bother to point out to Gwen that she'd just returned from a four-hour lunch break or that, most of the time, she sequestered herself in her office for the rest of the day. That would make things worse for sure. Instead, Brianna told her the truth.

"The reporter talked to Mr. Raeburn last week. She called back to let me know she was following up with Sara Shaw."

At the mention of the attorney's name, Gwen paled. Brianna would have loved to know what the story was, but she knew that was off limits. Tucking away the incident for future reference, Brianna couldn't help herself. "The reporter wanted to get my name as well—for the article."

Gwen's deer-in-the-headlights expression gave Brianna a surge of satisfaction. There would be consequences for her comment, but it was worth seeing Gwen taken off guard.

The woman's eyes narrowed, and she pointed at the stack of files on Brianna's desk. "Those need to be put away before you leave today." She swiveled on her heels so fast the shopping bags bounced into Brianna's desk, the sound of shoes hitting a cardboard box making it obvious what Gwen had purchased.

Brianna shook off Gwen's negativity and turned to her work. Maybe if she worked really hard she could buy expensive shoes, too.

Chapter 21

Cynthia asked herself for the twentieth time what had made her offer to talk to Sara on Brianna's behalf. An even better question was, Why did Brianna have to think about it? Cynthia believed Brianna's statement that someone was in the office. But still, she was doing Brianna a favor for even offering.

She looked down at her desk and shook her head. She had enough on her plate without getting involved in someone else's issues. But she hadn't expected to learn that the woman who had broken up Doug and Tasha's marriage was now working with Sara.

"Knock, knock."

Cynthia jumped at the sound of the voice. She looked up and saw Helene standing in the doorway wearing a sky-blue silk shirt paired with ivory linen pants. The look of excitement on Helene's face told Cynthia they were about to discuss another idea for Helene's wedding column. Cynthia's own dateless existence seemed even more bleak when she heard about plans for other people's weddings.

Stuffing down her own feelings, Cynthia smiled. "Hi, Helene. How are you this afternoon?"

The woman breezed into the office. She settled herself in a chair and put her purse down next to her. Helene leaned down to her purse and sat back up with a pen and a notebook.

"Fabulous. Tasha is back from her honeymoon. She and Greg loved the Maldives." Helene flipped through several pages in the notebook until she uncovered a bright-pink bookmark. "I'd like to expand the weekly column to include honeymoon tips. Listening to Tasha and Greg talk reminded me the honeymoon is as important as the wedding."

Cynthia knew a great idea when she heard one. Her editor would be thrilled with Helene's concept, and they might even be able to get the local travel agency to buy a large advertisement in that week's paper.

But the thought of reading about someone else's honeymoon made her stomach roll. Single people didn't want to hear what couples were doing. At least *she* didn't. But hers was only one opinion, and Cynthia decided to keep an open mind.

She listened to Helene's plans for the column and admitted it was a fully thought-through article. Not only had Helene convinced the travel agency to place an ad, but she'd also gotten them to sponsor a contest. One lucky couple would get two round-trip plane tickets to Las Vegas.

"This would be great for a honeymoon," Helene explained. "Or we could tie it into my article on eloping. Have you finished editing that, by the way? I want to make some changes to it. Did you know there are fifty chapels in Vegas? I only highlighted the ten with the best online reviews. That's what people your age look for these days, right?"

Cynthia nodded and picked up the article she'd covered in red ink. The draft looked like it was bleeding, but it was an improvement over Helene's previous first drafts. She handed it to Helene, who nodded.

"I'm getting better. I can see white paper beneath the red ink."

Helene's calm response surprised Cynthia. Ever since

Helene and her husband, Max, had gone to a therapist, she never reacted negatively to anything. Even the day that Evelyn Gerome, Helene's long-time rival, had gotten the last pumpkin spice latte at Betty's Coffee Shop, Helene was cool as a cucumber. Come to think of it, Helene was getting along with both of her daughters as well. Maybe she could give Cynthia some advice about how to deal with her mother's ultimatum to get out of the house.

"Can I ask you a personal question?" Cynthia said.

Helene frowned. "Don't you want to hear more about the column?"

"I do, but I need some advice, and you might be able to help me."

"I'd love to." Helene placed the papers on her lap and folded her hands on top of them. "Go ahead. What's on your mind?"

Positive that phrase had come straight from the therapist, Cynthia squirmed in her seat. Maybe it wasn't a good idea talking to her mother's friend, but she'd already opened her mouth. She might as well see if Helene had anything helpful to offer.

"I'm not sure if you know, but my mother has asked me to move out of the house."

Helene nodded and clapped her hands together. "Oh yes. We are excited! The Bunco Group, that is. There're twelve of us. Cybil thought she could start with that group and then branch out. Your mother promised us pottery lessons. Our first project is a dinner plate. That will weed out the less creative women and the ones who don't like to cook. God willing, Evelyn will be one of them. Once she knows who's really serious, Cybil plans to order pottery wheels and we'll move on to something more exciting like a mug or a vase. Your mom is giving me a discount on lessons because I promised to include her in a story about how to make your own wedding gifts."

Cynthia slumped back in her chair as the news sank in.

She knew about her mother's desire for a pottery studio, but she didn't know Cybil already had business plans for classes.

"Oh dear. You didn't know about this, did you?" Helene leaned forward and patted Cynthia's hand. "I should know by now to keep my mouth shut."

"No. I need to hear this. Mom told me some of it, but the extent of her plans is surprising, that's all."

"Do you have any leads on a new place yet?"

Shaking her head, Cynthia said, "Not a lot of places around here."

Helene sighed before she dug into her purse. She pulled out a business card and handed it over. Cynthia expected to see a real estate agent's number, but instead it was for a family therapist, Dr. Austen.

"This woman taught me how to communicate with my husband and daughters. If you want to improve your relationship with your mom, give her a call. But since you asked for my advice, let me say this: I was too involved in both Tasha's and Sara's lives. They suffered from my meddling and interfering. Tasha's wedding was almost ruined by all my silly ideas. Can you imagine what would have happened if they had let me rent an elephant to carry Greg to the church?"

Helene gathered up her papers and slid them into her purse before she continued.

"But I'm staying out of Sara's relationship. When she's ready to tell me about it, she will. Or she won't. I might be one of those mothers who gets a phone call from Vegas telling me I have a new son-in-law. If that's what Sara wants, it's her life.

"But, Cynthia, you should talk to your mother. Let her know if you need more time. We're all excited to start pottery classes, but we can wait."

Cynthia stood up with Helene and followed her to the door.

"I'll work on the edits of this week's column and get them

back to you tomorrow. Is it okay to start on the honeymoon article?" asked Helene.

"Sure. You're ahead of schedule. Whatever you want to write is fine."

Helene stopped at the door and turned to face Cynthia. "You'll figure out the housing situation. But please talk to your mother. She isn't a mind reader. Oh, and why don't you give Thomas Radcliffe a call? He's the relationship coordinator I tried to get Sara to use." Cynthia started to protest, but Helene winked. "Hold on. I'm not recommending you look for a date. I happen to know Thomas's latest love match moved in together, which means there's a house for rent somewhere around town. Call Thomas and you might get first dibs."

Cynthia watched Helene swish out of the office before shaking her head. Never in a million years would she come up with an idea like that. Leave it to Helene to think outside the box. Before she lost any time, Cynthia rushed back to her desk and dialed Thomas's number.

Chapter 22

"That wasn't on the list," Brianna said to the salesperson. She'd been on the phone for an hour trying to figure out what had happened. The latest shipment of furnishings for Raeburn's apartments had come in, but nothing was right. It was a downgrade in quality of everything they needed. It wasn't even close to the items she'd originally requested.

She glanced down at the printout of what she had submitted, lying next to the invoice of what was shipped. The same types of items were there, but the quality wasn't. Something had happened between the time she'd placed the order and the time it was shipped.

Brianna didn't want to ask for help. Gwen had made it clear her work had to be perfect or there would be an issue. It looked like she'd made a huge mistake, but Brianna didn't know how it could get this messed up.

"Lady, I don't know what you did, but we sent what made it to our system. Besides, this is your usual order. Why complain now about the same stuff you've gotten ten times before?"

She straightened up. "Wait. According to my records, we've never gotten anything like this. I copied and pasted our previous orders into the system. I've never even heard of the brand names you sent this time."

Brianna heard yelling in the background. The salesperson she was talking with shouted back, a creative use of obscenities that Alex would have been proud of, before returning to their conversation. "Look, I know you're new," he said. "Frankly, you're a hell of a lot easier to work with than that other woman."

Brianna nodded silently in agreement. Over the last month, Brianna had discovered Gwen's darker side. If anything went awry, the woman had a fit. Brianna didn't know how Raeburn put up with it, but she suspected he never saw that side of his property manager.

"You were a pleasure to chat with the other day," he continued.

She shook her head. "Hold on. This is the first time I've talked to you. I submitted everything electronically. Why would I call you?"

"You said you entered the wrong thing. I wrote it down."

Brianna heard paper moving and wondered what kind of company would still use paper if they had an online ordering system. Considering the situation, it might help her in the long run, though. She would be able to figure out what had happened to her order.

"Here it is," he announced. "You canceled the online order number 8034 and replaced it with your usual one. Said your name was Brianna Thompson, and you were taking over for Gwen."

Looking at the phone in her hand, Brianna couldn't decide if she was offended by the accusation or thankful he liked her better than Gwen. If this was any indication of how her job would be going, though, it looked like it was an uphill battle. No one was going to take her seriously if Gwen was going behind her back.

"Do I sound like the person you talked to the other day?"

Nothing about her voice reminded Brianna of Gwen, and she didn't see how they could be mistaken. This sales guy had spoken to Gwen for years. He should be able to tell the difference, shouldn't he?

"No. You don't. But I don't have time to argue about this. The order you received is the one you placed. If you don't like it, you can go through returns and ship it back. But I'm telling you right now that what you got is what you ordered, and I've got a record of you canceling the other order. Whatever you're up to, I'm not getting involved."

The line went dead, and Brianna put down the phone. What was she supposed to do now? The error put a crimp in the schedule, and it was the first time she'd been in charge of furnishing an apartment. She wanted things perfect for Ashley, Vanessa, Wesley, and their mom. The family held a special place in her heart since they were the first family she'd ever interviewed. If the place wasn't furnished, they'd have nowhere to go. And there wasn't time to place another order and get it down correctly.

Brianna sighed. She needed to talk to Gwen and find out what had happened. She started toward her boss's office when she remembered the other issue she needed to address with her. Turning around, Brianna grabbed the paperwork for the next round of tenants before heading to what she'd dubbed "Phoney France," her nickname for Gwen's office.

Knocking on the door, she waited for Gwen's gruff, "Enter," before she opened the door. Brianna kept her eyes focused on Gwen. She felt claustrophobic, surrounded by replicas of the Eiffel Tower.

"What?"

Gwen's standard greeting made her nervous. The screw-up with the furniture might set her over the edge. Brianna decided to start with the tenant question.

"I reviewed the new tenant list you left on my desk. I think there's been a mistake."

Gwen's left eyebrow arched, but she remained silent.

Brianna hesitated. She'd learned Gwen's silence meant she disagreed. Brianna shifted from one foot to the other before continuing. She needed to proceed with caution.

"The single woman, Lorraine, got an apartment, but not Suzanne."

"So?"

Gwen's short answer made Brianna nervous. "Well, I'm not sure if you remember, but Suzanne has five kids and a restraining order against her husband." Brianna paused and looked down at the paperwork. "Based on Mr. Raeburn's guidelines, Suzanne's needs outweigh Lorraine's. She should get an apartment this round."

Her boss stood up and tugged at the hem of her black dress. Brianna had come to think of Gwen's monochromatic wardrobe as a backdrop for the main event: the shoes. Minimum of three-inch heels, all designer and never, ever reworn. The shoes were the feature of the outfit.

"Maybe," said Gwen as she walked to one of the café chairs. She leaned against it and crossed her arms over her chest. "But the guidelines are subjective."

Brianna frowned. From the tone of Gwen's voice and the way she stood ready for a fight, Brianna knew she wasn't going to like what came next.

"For example, Lorraine doesn't have kids." Gwen paused, as if daring Brianna to interrupt.

Brianna bit her tongue to keep from spitting out that children needed stable, safe homes, which was what Raeburn's program offered.

"Second, Lorraine interviewed much better than Suzanne."

This time, Brianna couldn't keep quiet. "Suzanne was frazzled from her boys' argument." Suzanne's seven-year-old and nine-year-old sons had begun fighting the minute they walked into the office. Apparently, Suzanne had told them they would have to share a bedroom on the way to the interview. The boys thought they were entitled to their own rooms and made it a point to tell everyone who would listen about it. "But that shouldn't be counted against her."

"I have to take into account all aspects of the tenant's life. Suzanne can't keep her kids under control. Can you imagine the damage those boys could do to that apartment?" Brianna opened her mouth to respond, but Gwen held up a hand. "We can't help everyone. Sometimes people have to address their own issues before someone else can help them."

"Suzanne addressed her issues. She got the restraining order."

"The damage was done. The boys are problematic. Look, you might not like it, but this is a business. We have to make sure the apartments can be rented out for the long term. If we go with our hearts, then we won't have a job later on down the line because the money will have to be used to replace walls and doors and windows. Is that what you want?"

Gwen's argument made sense, but Brianna didn't like it. Or it could be she didn't like Lorraine. The woman was cold. Not professional, just cold. Gwen had her quirks, and the all-black, Francophile thing didn't send out warm fuzzies, but at least Gwen had passion about something.

This time, Brianna thought Gwen's passion was going in the wrong direction.

"We should help the people who need it the most. You saw Lorraine's financials compared to Suzanne's. Where else is a mother of five going to live when she's dependent on an abusive husband who can't hold down a job? He pulls in"— Brianna glanced at Suzanne's application—"forty-five thousand a year. If he stays employed, which, based on previous years, he won't. He's given her a whopping five hundred dollars in child support in the last five months. She's living in her car, which is probably going to be repossessed. Lorraine has a steady job and no dependents. Explain this to me."

Brianna took Gwen's perfectly pursed lips to be an indication that the conversation had veered in the wrong direction. Her assumption was confirmed when she heard Gwen's cold, haughty tone.

"Lorraine's had challenges as well. You may not see them right now, but she gets the apartment. End of discussion."

The finality of the statement told Brianna everything she needed to know. It was also clear now was not a good time to address the furniture situation. She'd have to figure it out on her own.

Chapter 23

A nagging suspicion plagued Brianna the entire weekend. She took another set of invoices and receipts home to reconcile and discovered another vendor, this time a window coverings company, with no documentation. No way would she mention it to Gwen, though. Her boss would be furious she hadn't paid the invoices in the first place.

In addition to that, she still couldn't get the bank account to reconcile. She knew she was missing something, but she couldn't figure out what.

Brianna scrunched up her face as she considered her options. Gwen had made it clear that she didn't want to be bothered by anything as mundane as basic accounting. Brianna could go to Raeburn—that was her preference—but going over Gwen's head would be another argument waiting to happen.

If she talked to Raeburn, she could bring up Suzanne's situation as well. It still bothered her that a mother of five and her children remained in a beat-up station wagon while Lorraine moved into an apartment even nicer than the one she currently had. That wasn't the point of the Women's Shelter and Support Agency.

At least Brianna had straightened out the mess with Ashley, Vanessa, and Wesley's apartment. The kids and their mother had moved into their fully furnished apartment last week. It had taken several late nights, but because she'd kept all her documentation, the furnishings store had relented. An apartment full of couches, beds, tables, and accessories arrived before the kids and their mom.

"Too bad replacing *my* stuff isn't as easy," she muttered to herself as she glanced around the living room. Philomena perched on the laundry basket Kevin had given her. A floor lamp that Kevin no longer needed sat next to it, as well as a worn leather armchair she'd found at a thrift shop. The insurance agency had promised a check for her stolen items in the next week, but Brianna hadn't been able to wait. Sitting on the floor with her work spread out gave her a lot of room but wasn't the most comfortable. "Maybe I should buy some cushions."

She spent the next few hours studying the numbers in front of her until, at noon, she heard a knock on her door. Brianna hopped up, glad for the break. Kevin and Rosemary had promised to drop by sometime this weekend. Rosemary had warmed up to her after they'd worked puzzles a few more times, and Kevin turned out to be as good a friend as she'd ever had. Granted, he was a cute male friend, but she focused on the fact that they had a good time together and not that he was male. Or cute. At least most of the time.

"Hurry up, Brianna," called out Rosemary. "It's heavy."

Brianna rushed to the door and flung it open. She frowned at the sight waiting for her in the hallway.

Rosemary held a wooden chair. It matched a small table in front of her door, as well as the chair Kevin held in his hands.

"Surprise!" Kevin called out. "Rosemary found you some more furniture."

"I'm tired of doing puzzles on the floor, so I started looking online for a table big enough," said Rosemary as she walked into the apartment. "Did you know there are tons of places you can get good furniture for really cheap?"

Kevin put down the chair he was holding and picked up the table.

"Let me help you," said Brianna. "You shouldn't do this by yourself."

She grabbed the opposite side of the table and immediately winced at the weight. How Kevin had managed to carry this himself was a mystery, but now that she'd committed to helping, she steeled her face and backed into her apartment.

"I think it should go there, by the window," said Rosemary. "Natural light is good for doing puzzles."

Brianna didn't know if that was true or not, but she didn't have the strength to move the table further. She and Kevin turned it to fit the long way against the wall and set it down. She took a closer look at it and ran her hand over the top. A rich, dark stain covered the smooth tabletop. Its quality reminded her of the table she'd had in her house in Saint Thomas. That one had cost a fortune, and she looked up at Kevin with concern. She had enough money to live on, but until the reimbursement check came, her finances were tight.

"Kevin," she started, "I'll pay you back. I promise. But it's going to take some time."

He shook his head. "No problem. If you don't like it, I can take it back. There were three other people who wanted it, but Rose and I got there first. And paid cash." He handed her a receipt, which was far less than she'd expected. "Pay me when you can."

"Wow! I can pay you right now!"

She headed to the kitchen for her purse and called over her shoulder, "Do you want anything to drink? Rosemary, I bought the juice boxes you like. Kevin?"

Rosemary followed her into the kitchen and helped herself to a juice box from the fridge. "Do you really like the table? Dad didn't know if you would."

Brianna glanced up at Rosemary after she found her wallet. "It's great. I had one similar to it a long time ago." She'd spent enough time with Rosemary to know the girl wanted affirmation she'd done the right thing. "You've got good taste."

The girl glowed with contentment. "I brought a new puzzle to test out. I'll meet you at the table."

Rosemary ran out of the room and straight into Kevin. He caught her in his arms and shook his head.

"From the looks of the papers on the floor, I think Brianna may be too busy for a puzzle, honey. We can come back another time. You've got homework to do anyway."

Rosemary's face fell, and Brianna chimed in, "I'm due for a break. Does Rosemary have time to get the outline of the puzzle started?—or finished, as fast as she works?"

"Please, Dad!" Rosemary pleaded. "I only have ten math problems left. Those won't take long. Please. Brianna needs a break. We'd be doing her a favor."

Brianna listened as Rosemary negotiated with her father. They playfully argued back and forth. The love in his eyes shone through. Brianna's breath hitched for a second. What would it be like to have someone look at her like that? Unconditional love from a responsible, caring partner? Brianna couldn't remember feeling something like that from anyone she'd dated.

"Fine. But it's the outline of the puzzle only or thirty minutes—whichever comes first."

Rosemary pumped her arm in the air and ran to the table, where she dumped out the puzzle pieces.

Brianna blinked back her thoughts and smiled at Kevin when he asked, "You okay?"

"Fine. Thinking about my work puzzle. Not as much fun as Rosemary's kind." She nodded toward the coffeepot. "Care for a cup? The guy who gave it to me has excellent taste in coffee."

Kevin laughed and shook his head. "I've had my two cups for the day, but thanks."

Brianna fished around in her wallet and pulled out the money for the table. "Here you go," she said, and handed the bills to him. "Impressive find, by the way."

Kevin tucked the money into his back pocket as they walked into the living room. By the time they made it to the table, Rosemary had already finished one side of the puzzle.

"She found it on her own. I had no idea she was a bargain hunter," Kevin said as he tapped on the solid wood furniture. He turned to Rosemary. "If you don't slow down, we'll be out of here in five minutes."

Rosemary rolled her eyes. "I'll have this thing finished in less than thirty minutes," she said, and went back to work.

Kevin watched his daughter put two pieces together, then pointed at the papers on the floor. "What are you doing with all this?"

Now that she was over the excitement of getting a new table, Brianna remembered her problem. "Just some work stuff. Reconciling bills."

Kevin picked up an invoice and looked at it. "Rosemary was telling me you want to be a forensic accountant. Any truth to that story?"

She shook her head as she gathered up the receipts from the floor and put them in a pile. "I'm studying for my real estate license. The accounting stuff is part of the day job I've got to pay the bills until I pass my test."

He handed her the invoice. "Well, if you need any help with that, let me know. I paid my way through college doing admin work for a lumber yard. I still dream about making collection calls for accounts receivable."

Brianna laughed. "Wouldn't that classify as a nightmare?"

"I suppose it could be. But if you need any help, let me know. I'm pretty good with numbers."

She thanked him for the offer but declined. Kevin cleared

his throat and looked down at his shoes. Brianna wracked her brain for something to get the conversation flowing again when she remembered the copy of the newspaper stuffed in with the kitchen supplies.

"Hey, random question: Where did you get the newspaper that was packed in the boxes?" When he didn't respond immediately, she added, "It was from a small town. Glen Valley. It's off the beaten path."

Her comment was rewarded with a nod. "That's the understatement of the year. I'm surprised you've heard of it."

She hesitated before answering. "I worked there briefly when I was transitioning to Vegas."

Brianna thought Kevin would be curious, but instead, his face clouded. "Linda's parents were from that area. They got her a subscription to keep in touch with what was going on. I haven't had the heart to ask them to cancel it."

She cringed at the thought that Kevin might know Doug, but it didn't seem to matter. Rather than continue the conversation, Kevin wandered over to watch his daughter work the puzzle. As she watched Kevin, it was clear that he was still grieving the loss of his wife.

Chapter 24

She didn't see Kevin or Rosemary much that week. Brianna missed doing puzzles with Rosemary, but she focused on the missing receipts. She hadn't made any progress other than to discover another $16,000 difference. After three more days of searching, Brianna put aside the reports and prepared for a full day of interviews.

At the end of the day on Wednesday, Brianna showed the last interviewee out the front door. "I'll give you a call in a few days to let you know. Thanks for coming in to meet with us."

She locked the door behind the woman and rested her forehead on the cool metal. This was the toughest interview she'd done yet this week. The woman's situation was awful, but based on the guidelines, Brianna doubted she would get one of the coveted apartments. Combined with the fact that Brianna was no closer to figuring out the accounts payable issue, she was tired and cranky and wanted to go home.

Her head jerked at the sound of Gwen's voice.

"I have to admit you did a great job in that last interview. I didn't think you had it in you."

Gwen's compliment confused her. The woman had been hot and cold all week. It pleased Brianna that Gwen knew how hard she was working, but considering the situation, it also made her sad. The potential resident had been traumatized by her ex-husband to the point it was difficult for her to hold a conversation. Brianna spent the entire session asking questions in her most soothing voice, never letting on her surprise when the woman told her about the horrible things her ex had done.

At least Doug wasn't that big of an ass, she thought on several occasions.

"How do you do this and not let it get you down?" she asked as she turned back to her boss. Brianna didn't intend to share anything personal, but it slipped out. "I've had a lot of bad experiences with men, but nothing compared to that."

When Gwen didn't answer immediately, Brianna decided she'd overstepped her bounds. A truce between the two of them worked for her. She didn't need a friend in her boss. It was clear who was in charge, and Brianna's question appeared to have crossed the line.

Brianna didn't wait for an answer and went to her desk to finish up the day's paperwork. She'd been rushing through it this week so she could get home and work a puzzle with Rosemary. But tonight was parent-teacher conferences, and Kevin and Rosemary wouldn't be home until later. Brianna settled into her chair to sort out the applications and enter them into the computer when Gwen spoke.

"On nights like this, I usually go out for a drink."

Brianna's head whipped toward Gwen in surprise.

Gwen gave her a rueful grin. "Didn't think I was human, did you?"

"It's not that." Brianna scrambled to come up with a response, but Gwen was right. Her boss never flinched when hard decisions had to be made. Brianna thought again about Suzanne and her five kids. She doubted Gwen had given them a second thought. The fact that today's interview had bothered Gwen might be proof she had emotions. "Well, maybe I thought you'd done this long enough that you had a trick for keeping the stories from bothering you."

"Alcohol is the best trick I've found." Gwen disappeared into her office and came right out with her purse in her hand. "Come on. I know a place close to here."

Brianna looked down at the paperwork in front of her. "I need to finish this. It'll only take a couple minutes."

"Leave it. It can wait."

Unsure this was the best decision, Brianna powered down the computer, grabbed her purse, and followed Gwen out of the office.

After Gwen set the alarm, the two women walked in silence down the sidewalk. Brianna caught several men staring at Gwen, who ignored them and continued on her way. Brianna struggled to keep up, even though she wore flats compared to Gwen's stilettos.

How the hell does she walk in those heels? Her feet have to hurt!

By the time Gwen pointed at a bright-red door with a picture of a piano on it, Brianna was breathing hard.

"Do you sing?" Gwen asked not the least bit winded from the walk.

Brianna's eyes grew wide. Even when she could breathe, singing wasn't her jam. She inhaled deeply to catch her breath and mumbled, "Not if I can help it."

Gwen's eyebrows arched, and she smiled. Something Brianna hadn't seen until now.

"Then tonight will be fun."

The bouncer, a man with bulging biceps that fought to be free of his tight black T-shirt, perked up at Gwen's approach.

"You're back. The place is boring when you aren't around." He nodded at Brianna and asked, "This your new partner?"

"We'll see," Gwen said. "She says she doesn't sing."

Brianna swore the muscles in the man's biceps grew before her eyes.

"If she can't back you up, there're a couple of regulars in tonight. You'll be fine."

Gwen handed him $20, but he shook his head. "On the house. We need good tunes."

He ushered her through the door, but when Brianna started to follow, he stepped in front of her. "Cover charge is twenty bucks."

Brianna wished now that she had stayed at the office and worked. While she had some spending cash, she didn't want to waste it on a cover charge. She handed it over to the man as Gwen stuck her head out the door.

"Really, Jesse. She's with me. Let her in."

He scowled before he returned the money and let Brianna pass.

She halted as soon as she walked through the door to let her eyes adjust to the low light, then took in her surroundings. The bar didn't resemble anything she expected from the run-down exterior. Purple lights glowed from the bar, highlighting the metal-and-glass structure. It was a perfect fit in Las Vegas. The mirrors behind the liquor bottles reflected the light out onto the tables, which faced a raised dais where a piano snuggled up to a large black box, which Brianna recognized as a karaoke machine. A few people sat at the tables, but most were crowded around the bar.

Gwen strode straight to the far end of the bar, where two barstools sat vacant. She stopped short of the seat when she turned back. She waved at Brianna. "Hurry up. We don't have a lot of time."

Not sure what was so urgent, Brianna made her way to the bar and watched as Gwen tossed her purse behind it. She reached back for Brianna's. When Brianna hesitated, Gwen shook her head. "You can't karaoke with a purse. Hand it over."

Letting up a silent prayer that no one would steal her meager possessions, she handed it to Gwen, who chucked it next to her own. Then Gwen called out to the woman behind the bar, "Two specials, Rhiane. And make it snappy." She sat down on a barstool and patted the one next to it. "Sit down. Best to pick your songs early. Any you prefer?"

"I can't sing, remember?" said Brianna.

Gwen left her at the bar and headed toward the karaoke machine. It didn't appear to matter that this wasn't what Brianna wanted to do. It went hand-in-hand with a drink.

The bartender placed two copper mugs in front of her. "Two specials, twenty-five dollars." The woman waited, as if she were expecting Brianna to pay.

"Rhiane, right?"

The woman's chin dropped slightly as she crossed her arms over the black T-shirt with its carelessly removed sleeves. One bicep boasted a tattoo of a large-chested siren lounging on a rock. The creature's face was calm and peaceful as she waved to a boat full of men passing by. Rhiane's other bicep showed the same siren, this time picking her teeth with what looked like a bone. Splinters of wood and sails floated in the water around her.

Best not mess with this one, Brianna thought. "My purse is behind the counter. Gwen tossed it with hers."

Before she could finish, Gwen slapped a notebook on the table. "Thanks, Rhiane. Put them on my tab."

Without a word, the woman turned and went to the far end of the bar.

Brianna looked down at her drink. A brownish liquid filled the mug, which was garnished by an orange. "What is this?"

"The special."

Brianna picked up the mug and sniffed. She closed one eye as a powerful aroma hit her nose. "I heard that. But what's actually in it? Smells like bourbon."

Gwen didn't look up from the notebook when she said, "It's the special. It changes every night. Whatever surplus liquor they have, they use. Keeps costs down and they can charge an obscene amount for it." She grabbed her mug, took a swig, and grimaced. "Tequila. Lots of it."

Taking a small sip, Brianna agreed with Gwen's assessment. She made a mental note to only have one if she wanted to get to work on time in the morning. She leaned over to see the notebook Gwen was studying.

"Do they have anything other than eighties hair bands?"

Gwen looked up and smiled. "Yes, they do."

THREE HOURS and two specials later, Brianna staggered back to the bar from the karaoke stage. Her throat was parched from belting out country tunes. It was amazing what a little tequila could do for one's singing ability. Or maybe it was the tequila that altered her judgement. Tonight, Brianna sounded like a rock star.

"Another special, Rhiane," Brianna called out as she slid onto a barstool.

The bartender turned toward her and shook her head. "Water's on its way."

Gwen plunked down next to her. "Don't you dare do that. Another special for my friend. And one for me."

Brianna propped her elbow on the sticky bar and rested her head in hand. "Is it a good idea for us to be doing this? You're my boss, remember?" Her head slid off her hand, and Brianna barely stopped her head from hitting the counter. To cover up her drunkenness, she sat up straight and pointed at Gwen. "What if you have to fire me?"

Gwen leaned back and straightened the skirt of her ever-present black outfit. "You gonna do something stupid to get fired?"

"Don't plan on it. But I didn't plan to fall in love with an idiot who would make me quit my dream job." Brianna blinked as she realized what she'd said. This was the first time she'd ever told anyone the truth about why she left Saint Thomas. Doug knew, but he'd caused it.

"I wondered what your story was."

Rhiane slammed down two glasses of water in front of them.

Gwen snarled, "I said specials."

"Water, then another special. You'll bitch up a storm about your hangover if you don't hydrate."

Gwen waved a finger at Rhiane's back as the bartender walked away, then swayed to the left before she righted herself and focused on Brianna. "So. Love gone wrong. Out with it."

Maybe it was the alcohol or maybe it was the fact she was lonely, but Brianna confessed. "I was a real estate agent in Saint Thomas. A good one. Loved my job. Adored the island. What I wouldn't do to go back there." She took a sip of the water and let it soothe her throat. As much as she didn't want Rhiane telling her what to do, the water was a good idea. Her head felt muddled, and she knew morning would come far too soon. "But I let a man take away my options. And my money."

Gwen grunted in agreement as she drained her water glass and slammed in on the counter. "Never let 'em know you have more money than them. That scares 'em off every time."

Brianna gave a half grin. "It wasn't that. He had way more money than me. His wife—"

Her boss interrupted. "He was married? Now it gets juicy. This calls for another round." Gwen waved down at Rhiane. "Hey, two more specials and some more water." She turned to face Brianna and motioned with her hands to continue. "Let's hear it. Spare no details."

Shaking her head, Brianna decided neither she nor Gwen would remember much of this in the morning, so she started from the beginning.

"He came to town looking for a second home. He and his *ex*-wife had won the lottery, and the sky was the limit. I sold him a beautiful beachfront property. Modern, with an infinity-edge pool. All the bells and whistles a smart house could offer."

"Sounds pricey." Gwen glared at Rhiane when the bartender placed another water in front of each of them, but the bartender gave a curt nod and walked away. "What could go wrong with that?"

Brianna sipped the water, glad that Rhiane had ignored Gwen. Probably for the best. "To begin with, the douche—"

Gwen spit out her water, dousing the bar. "That's his nickname? Lead with that next time. It will make for a better story."

Rhiane stomped over to their section of the bar and wiped it down with a dingy rag. "Pull it together, Gwen."

Gwen raised her hand in protest. "Not my fault." She pointed at Brianna. "This one is telling stories about her ex-boyfriend. You'll never guess what his name was."

Rhiane rolled her eyes and shook her head before turning toward the other end of the bar.

"Your loss," Gwen called after her. She blinked her eyes several times as if she were having problems focusing, then swiveled her barstool to face Brianna. "Go on with the douche."

Brianna giggled. Hearing Gwen utter Doug's nickname seemed out of character. It should have been a warning, but she continued.

"Turns out he wasn't divorced. And he had kids. Cute ones, actually. Well, sort of. . . . They ID'd me when I showed up to work for their aunt. That wasn't a lot of fun, but I did get to deck him that day. But then their aunt pulled my hair." Brianna rubbed her head at the memory. "It still doesn't grow right in that spot."

Gwen's face crunched together. "Hold on. I thought we were talking about The Douche."

Taking another sip of water, Brianna said, "We are. That's

background information. Let me focus." She stared at the dartboard in an effort to make the room stop spinning. "So, The Douche was married with kids when we met. His wife thought he was buying a vacation home, but he was already planning to leave her. I happened to be the real estate agent who showed him the house and ended up dating him."

Gwen lurched forward, and Brianna's arm shot out to catch her. Pushing her back into place, Brianna giggled. "You might have had too much to drink."

Shaking her head, Gwen squirmed back onto her barstool. "No. It's not that. You're not supposed to date a client. Didn't you know that?"

The warm, fuzzy feeling in Brianna's head disappeared, and a dull ache replaced it. It had all happened years ago, but it still irritated her that she had let Doug end her career. She went on the defensive.

"We didn't date until after the house closed. I found out after we moved in together that he was married."

"Why didn't you split then?"

Brianna had asked herself the same question many times before. If she had never moved in with Doug, she would still be selling real estate in paradise. But now she was singing karaoke with her drunk boss in Las Vegas. Something didn't seem right about that. She told Gwen what she told everyone who asked.

"He was fun and exciting. We went out all the time. He had plenty of money. At least until he spent it all. I'm nothing like his ex-wife, and I don't want kids. He pretended that the kids were his wife's idea, but I found out later that was all him. He even tried to choose their gender."

Gwen's eyes opened wide. Brianna didn't know if it was because she didn't believe what she was hearing or because she was drunk and having trouble seeing.

"You can do that?"

"If you find the right doctor, sure." Brianna took a large

gulp of water. Talking about Doug made her thirsty. "Anyway, things went well for a while. Parties and vacations and shopping trips. A new car. You name it, he gave it to me."

"How'd he get his money?"

"I told you. His ex won the lottery. The guy never worked a day we were together."

"So, then, why the hell aren't you still with him?"

Brianna grabbed her water and sipped. She hated this part of the story. She felt vulnerable, and people always looked at her differently after they knew. But it was the truth, and she couldn't run from it.

"He spent all his money on different business ventures, all of which went bust. When he blew through his money, he 'borrowed' mine, then attempted to use my real estate license without my knowledge. That's when I realized I needed to get out."

She was feeling sorry for herself when, all of a sudden, Gwen threw her arm around her shoulders and gave her a squeeze.

"Well, to hell with him. You're a great addition to our office, and you don't even need a license to work there." Gwen lifted her copper mug. "Let's make a toast. To dumping asshat boyfriends and making new friends."

It took her a minute to realize Gwen was serious. Or as serious as she could be while drunk. Maybe it was a good idea to open up to people. It felt like a weight had been lifted off her chest that she didn't know was there. Grabbing her glass of water, Brianna toasted with Gwen.

"To new friends." She grinned. "Does this mean I can come in late tomorrow morning?"

True to form, Gwen gave her the refined look she expected.

"Hell no. Eight sharp or I'll write you up."

Chapter 25

Brianna cradled her head in her hands. She cursed Rhiane's "specials." The drinks didn't leave her feeling special this morning, just hungover. Two cups of coffee and a full dose of ibuprofen helped, but the pounding in her head promised a long day.

Despite her less-than-optimal condition, she'd arrived in the office at 7:59 a.m. Brianna assumed Gwen would be sitting at her desk, making sure she was on time, but the office was quiet when she let herself in.

Lifting her head, she shoved the files from last night's interviews aside and booted up her computer. Brianna checked her voicemails while she waited. She sat up straighter as she listened to the message.

"Hi, this is Superior Furnishing. This message is for Brianna Thompson. Wanted to confirm the change order you sent last night. Good thing I was working late or I wouldn't have seen it in time. You might consider sending it in before midnight."

Brianna frowned. She'd been asleep in bed by eleven. She leaned forward to listen to the rest of the message.

"Despite your late request, I managed to cancel the existing furniture order and replace it with the new one you emailed over. I know we've

worked with Raeburn Property Management for years, but lady, the changes you keep making . . . Well, I don't wanna go over your head, but this has got to stop. Mr. Raeburn is a good guy, and what he's doing for these women is definitely needed. But I need more than a couple hours to make changes like this. This is the last time I can do it for you."

She checked the timestamp of the voicemail. The message had been left at seven this morning. Her computer chimed, signaling her to log in. As fast as she could, Brianna pulled up her email and looked through her messages. Sure enough, someone had sent an email from her account at 11:47 p.m., and Superior had responded by confirming the changes would be made.

Brianna downloaded the attachment. As she skimmed over it, her eyes narrowed. Someone had changed every item she'd ordered. Unlike the previous times, this order upgraded everything, tripling the cost of the invoice.

Her heart rate sped up. This order was for Lorraine's unit. Brianna had authorized payment before getting the final invoice because the woman insisted on moving in sooner than planned, and it was the only way to get the furniture store to agree. Brianna forced herself to take a deep breath before she continued reading the document. She blew out the breath to the count of four and repeated it. Maybe if she got a hold of herself, things would be fine.

The door opened while she was doing the breathing exercise, and she had a sinking feeling. Facing Gwen with a hangover and bad news would not go over well. Giving a silent prayer that the ibuprofen would kick in, she plastered a smile on her face to greet Gwen.

Only it wasn't Gwen. It was Mr. Raeburn.

"Good morning, Brianna. You're looking . . . ." He paused and did a double take. Brianna knew he was too nice to comment on her bedraggled appearance, but she knew she'd seen better days. He took a step back. "You look tired. Are you okay? Don't tell me you have the same stomach bug as Gwen.

She left me a message this morning that she won't be in. I was hoping you could cover for her today, but if you're sick . . ."

Brianna shook her head, then stopped when pain ricocheted through her skull. "No. I'm fine. Late night is all." She hoped this morning's shower had washed away the scent of tequila and sweat. Sitting as still as possible, she asked, "What can I do for you?"

Raeburn nodded at the computer. "Gwen sent me a list of things she planned to work on today. I'll forward the email to you. Please take care of them. She shouldn't have to worry while she's sick." He turned to walk to his office, then stopped. "Oh, and I'm expecting my partner, Jared, to drop by later this afternoon. Give me a call when he gets here."

Brianna swallowed back the bile that crept up her throat and closed her eyes when she heard Raeburn's door close. Seeing Jared wasn't something she looked forward to, but today of all days made it even worse. Last night had been a setup. She should have known better. Gwen didn't want to be her friend. She wanted someone to manipulate. Brianna shook her head when she thought about how well Gwen had played her.

She checked her computer. Gwen had access to her email, so it was possible she was responsible for the cancellation and the new order. It made sense. Gwen went out of her way to accommodate all of Lorraine's requests. Lorraine didn't even deserve an apartment let alone the type of furnishings she was getting.

Maybe Brianna should tell Raeburn what was happening instead of trying to figure it out herself. With Gwen out of the office, today would be the perfect day for it. She had the file folder of invoices and receipts that didn't add up, and she could print out the emails concerning Lorraine's apartment. Raeburn might be happy that she'd uncovered what Gwen was doing and give Suzanne the apartment. Cautiously optimistic, she proceeded to print the emails.

As she was tucking the printouts into her file folder with the other research, her computer dinged, signaling a new email. She checked her inbox and groaned. Raeburn had forwarded the list of things Gwen wanted done today. It would take her all day, and most of them didn't make any sense. Why would she relabel all the files for the program applicants? Gwen's note said the labels needed to be color-coded based on financial need. And the files needed to be changed to signify how many children would be living in each apartment.

"How stupid can you get?" she said aloud.

Brianna fumed at the waste of time before she calmed down enough to consider the options. Gwen wanted to put her in her place and prove she wasn't up to the job. She needed proof that Gwen had something to do with all the strange things that were happening. If Brianna went to Raeburn with complaints and no proof, she would look like a petty subordinate. Better to do what she was asked to do and gather more proof along the way.

Pleased with her decision, Brianna took a deep breath. She needed to get started if she wanted to hand something to Raeburn today, but the pounding in her head started again.

"Ibuprofen first, then detective work."

Chapter 26

Brianna fell back into her chair. It had taken most of the day, but she finished Gwen's to-do list. If she hadn't had to go to three office supply stores to find the exact shade of lilac labels Gwen requested, she would have been finished hours ago. Gwen must hate her to make her do such useless stuff. It was almost like she was working for Alex again. Alex did this sort of thing when he wanted to cover up a botched business deal.

She closed her eyes. Had she left one job to come to another that was doing illegal stuff, too? She didn't want to find another job. For the first time in her adult life, Brianna believed in what her employer did. Sure, selling real estate made money, but Raeburn Property Management made a difference in women's and children's lives.

Plus, the money was better than she'd made with Alex, and, despite Gwen, it was a more pleasant working environment. Brianna stretched her head from side to side. The tension she was feeling these days reminded her of the anxiety of Saint Thomas. The only difference was Doug wasn't here.

Or was he?

She'd been so busy the last few days that she'd pushed her grocery store experience to the back of her mind. Last time she went to the store, she could have sworn she saw Doug darting behind an end cap when she'd pulled a loaf of bread off the shelf. She'd hurried to the end of the aisle to see if her eyes had been playing tricks on her, but there was no one there. She couldn't help feeling like someone was following her, though.

Shaking the thought out of her head, Brianna told herself to stop being jittery and focus on the work. She was ready to present her concerns to Raeburn. He could help her figure out what to do.

Before she could stand up, the office door opened. Brianna remembered Raeburn had mentioned his partner planned to stop by.

"Waited too long," she mumbled under her breath before she plastered a professional smile on her face. She looked up and greeted the visitor. "Good afternoon. Welcome to Raeburn—"

The sentence remained unfinished when she saw Sara Shaw and Jared Hughes standing in front of her desk. Her mouth dried out. Even if she had known what to say, she couldn't speak. Even though she had every right to be in this office, Brianna couldn't help but tense up in Sara's presence.

It was Jared who finally spoke up. "Hello. I don't think we met properly last time." He offered his hand. "I'm Jared Hughes."

Brianna took his hand and shook it. She licked her lips and swallowed hard. "Brianna Thompson."

"Otherwise known as China, I believe."

She released his hand. "That was Doug's nickname for me. I don't use it anymore."

"Fair enough." He turned to Sara and put a hand on her waist. The gesture seemed intimate for coworkers, but Brianna could tell from the shock on Sara's face that she hadn't been expecting to see her. This must have been Jared's way of being supportive. "I'm sure you remember Sara Shaw. She works with me at the Miller Agency now."

Brianna rubbed one hand over the back of her head before extending the other hand. "Yes, I do."

Brianna's hand hung in space for a few seconds before Sara reacted. The lawyer cleared her throat and shook her hand. Brianna blinked at the tight grip. The pressure lasted for a few seconds before she extricated her extremity. Brianna glanced down at her hand. Sara was still not a fan.

She looked up when Sara said, "Carl's expecting us. I was hoping to talk to Gwen about the latest round of applicants to the Women's Shelter and Support Agency." Before Brianna could tell them Gwen wasn't available, Sara continued, "How long have you been working here? I didn't know Mr. Raeburn had replaced the receptionist."

"Carl told me," Jared said. Sara's eyes flickered, and Brianna suspected it was irritation directed at both Jared *and* her. "He mentioned he rescued someone from Alex Dunderblatt's office. I didn't think to ask for a name, but it makes sense."

"How does that make sense exactly?" Brianna asked, surprising herself. It felt confrontational to speak up, but today's turn of events had pushed her to the max. Softening her tone, she added, "Why would you have known I worked for Alex?"

The look Sara and Jared exchanged told Brianna she didn't want to know the answer. Brianna knew neither of them thought highly of her. She assumed Sara had told Jared about her bad judgement when it came to men. Even though Brianna hadn't dated Alex, it was bad judgement working for a man like that.

"Never mind," Brianna said. "It's none of my business. Ms. Martin isn't in today, but Mr. Raeburn is expecting you. You can wait here or in the conference room. Can I get you anything to drink?"

"We'd both love a bottle of water," said Jared.

As Brianna waited for Sara's response, Raeburn walked out into the reception area.

"Jared! Great to see you!" The men exchanged handshakes. "I was starting to think you stood me up today."

"Delayed flight. You know how it goes," said Jared. "Carl, let me introduce Sara Shaw. She's the newest member of the Miller Agency. She worked on the riverfront renovations in Glen Valley, and she's been working on your project here in Vegas."

Raeburn shook Sara's hand, then patted Jared's back. "Great to meet you in person. Let's head to my office. Jared and I can catch up and I can get to know Sara. It's important to know who's on your team." He smiled at Brianna. "Would you mind bringing us some refreshments?"

Brianna relaxed. All she needed to do was get some water for everyone, then Sara and Jared would be with Raeburn for the rest of the afternoon. She'd have to hold off talking to him about the discrepancies in the books, but she'd have time later.

Sara looked at her watch. "Actually, we've got an appointment at four thirty, and I was hoping to see one of the apartments. Jared's told me all about them, but I'd like to check one out for myself."

A funny feeling ran through Brianna, and she predicted Raeburn's next request.

Her boss turned to her. "You can pull something together for us, right? Gwen usually handles this sort of thing, but I'm sure she won't mind if you take them on a tour. I'll tag along in case you need any help."

Wishing he would do the tour himself, she knew she couldn't turn down the request. Brianna nodded.

"Let me pull the address and grab the key. It'll only take me a couple minutes." She pushed back from her chair. She needed a minute to calm herself before she could spend any more time with Sara. Without waiting for a response, Brianna hurried back to Gwen's door. Since her boss was out for the day, she didn't knock but went straight in.

She hadn't expected to find Gwen sitting behind her desk, but it was the man sitting in one of the café chairs that threw her for a loop. And it wasn't just any man.

It was Doug.

Chapter 27

"Fancy seeing you here." Doug smiled at his ex-girlfriend. He'd expected a similar response from her, but instead her face flushed. Feeling a bit put out, he started to ask her what was wrong when Gwen spoke up.

"You two know each other?"

Doug recognized the panic on Brianna's face as he processed the situation. As much as he'd wanted to find his ex, now wasn't a good time to reconcile with her. He'd learned a few things about Gwen since they made their deal at the Parisian Café. She was smart, and she mitigated risks. She had explained to him one day how Raeburn had hired an assistant without telling her. It put a crimp in her plans, but Gwen had figured out a way to blame the creative bookkeeping as well as renting to non-needy candidates on the new hire. If someone figured out Gwen was using the Women's Shelter and Support Agency as an ATM, it would look like the assistant had set the whole thing up.

Brianna was the fall guy.

A tiny shred of guilt wiggled its way into Doug's heart. He knew Gwen was as cutthroat as they came. He'd dealt with a lot of characters before, but no one held a candle to Gwen.

The ominous black clothing she wore made her look like she was dressed for a funeral, always prepared to take someone out. Vindictive and calculating were two adjectives that suited her to a tee.

But as much as he wanted Brianna, he needed Gwen. He needed the money.

Shaking his head, Doug said, "I saw her win a bunch of money at a slot machine a while back. That's all."

Brianna's eyes narrowed, then she smoothed down her shirt. The action drew attention to the pink poodles dancing across it. Only Brianna could wear a ridiculous outfit like that and still look beautiful.

Careful, Doug. Eyes on the prize. Money before women.

He turned his gaze to Gwen, who was studying him. He shrugged, hoping that would be the end of it. Gwen gave a slight shake of her head before she turned to Brianna. Doug noticed Brianna's rigid posture. She was more nervous than he was.

"Why are you barging in without knocking?" Gwen asked Brianna.

Doug let out a tiny breath. While he didn't want to see anything bad happen to Brianna, it was better that Gwen's attention was focused anywhere but on him. Especially when he heard what Brianna said next.

"Mr. Raeburn's in his office with some of the attorneys from the Miller Agency."

Doug stiffened at the name of the company that had ruined him. He glanced at Gwen and saw she didn't look happy about it either.

Brianna nodded toward the hallway. "Jared Hughes and Sara Shaw."

Doug grimaced. The mere mention of Jared and Sara's names caused him pain. He was still pissed off about losing the easy gig in Glen Valley, and he blamed both these lawyers for it.

Doug turned to Gwen. "I should leave," he said, and stood up.

"Sit down."

Gwen's cold tone sent a shiver down Doug's spine, but he shrugged it off. He walked to the door and grabbed the knob.

Brianna dashed to the door and leaned against it. "You can't go out there."

Doug glared back at her. "I seem to remember you not being interested in what I do anymore."

He pulled the knob again and managed to open the door a crack before Brianna leaned her weight against it. Doug pulled harder when Gwen whisper-screamed, "Stop! Close the door."

Doug whipped around to glare at Gwen, giving Brianna enough time to push the door shut. She settled herself in front of the handle, making it impossible for him to get out of the office unless he physically moved her. As angry as he was, violence wasn't the answer. At least not today.

Doug strode back across the office and put his hands on Gwen's desk. He leaned forward, getting as close to her face as the desk would allow. "I didn't sign up for this. Hughes is an asshat, and Sara Shaw . . . ," he spat out the name, "Shaw is the biggest bitch there is. Well, except for you, apparently."

Her eyes remained cold and focused, but Gwen's lips curved up in a smile. The expression made him squirm, especially when he realized he'd revealed more about his relationship with Brianna than he should have. And from the look on Gwen's face, he was going to have to deal with that slip immediately.

"So, you and Brianna just met?" she asked. "If that's the case, why would she know you can't be seen by the lawyers?"

He opened his mouth to tell her it was none of her business, but Gwen held up her hand.

"No. Don't tell me. I already know your background. Your sordid affair wasn't hard to dig up." She gestured to Brianna.

"I'm quite impressed with your fall from grace. Pretty impressive drop from accomplished real estate agent to receptionist." Gwen clasped her hands together and pointed at Doug. "And you. Brianna's right—you can't go out there. They see you and there will be questions."

Nerves made Doug's stomach clench, but he kept his face neutral. "So? I have as much right to be here as anyone else."

Gwen's severe bob didn't move as she shook her head. "No, you don't. And if I tell Raeburn who you are, you won't be allowed back in. And that's a problem for both of us, isn't it?"

Doug frowned. He didn't want Brianna to know he was working with Gwen, but she knew it. Focusing on Gwen, he noted self-satisfaction on her face. This woman was up to something.

"Fine. What do you propose I do now? Not like I can leave or anything."

"No. You can't." Gwen turned her attention to Brianna. "Why are *you* in my office?"

"Mr. Raeburn wants to show Jared and Sara one of the apartments. I offered to get keys since you're off sick today."

Doug's eyebrows raised in surprise. "Lying to the boss. Classy."

Gwen shot him a look that would make an ordinary man melt into a pool of goo, but Doug dropped back in his chair and tucked his hands behind his head. It was nice to see Gwen wasn't as perfect as she thought she was.

"I don't have a lot of time," said Brianna. "Sara has a meeting to get to. If they're going to tour an apartment, it needs to be now."

"That one is always on a schedule. She wouldn't know what to do with herself if she didn't have a bunch of meetings set up," said Gwen.

Doug couldn't help but agree with her. He remembered how upset Sara used to get anytime he and Tasha arrived late for dinner. He watched as Gwen opened her drawer and pulled out a key.

"Take them to 6 East Main. Unit 2B has been cleaned and will show well." Gwen glanced at her watch. "Did they say how much time they have?"

Brianna's fist tightened around the key. Doug watched as the tops of her knuckles turned white.

"Not much. They have another appointment at four thirty."

Gwen nodded and sat back in her chair. "Tag along. You can be my eyes and ears." Brianna started to speak, but Gwen cut her off. "Tell Carl I called in while you were getting the key. I asked you to go to the apartment. He won't question it."

Doug couldn't help but grin when he noticed the key poking through Brianna's first and second knuckles. If it were him, he might attack Gwen with the key, but he knew Brianna didn't have it in her. She was frustrated about having to do what she was told.

"Anything else you need me to do before I leave?" Brianna seethed.

Doug heard a touch of sarcasm in Brianna's voice and glanced over at Gwen to see if she caught it as well. Gwen focused on her computer, and she jabbed the keys hard and fast. She must have found what she wanted because her attention went back to Brianna.

"Or would you like to explain why you're in your office when you are supposed to be sick? And what he's doing here?"

Gwen ignored Brianna's questions and asked, "Are you finished with the work I left you?"

Brianna nodded; her lips pursed. Doug glanced at her hand again. The key was no longer in an offensive position. Considering she would be spending the next hour with Sara, that was a good thing.

"Shall I let Ms. Shaw and Mr. Hughes know you made it

into the office after all and can meet with them?" Brianna suggested.

Doug's eyes flew to Gwen's face. This time, Brianna's comment provoked a reaction. Gwen's face froze, reminding Doug of a stone statue. Her skin looked smooth and cold, as if she were incapable of any pleasant expression. He hadn't known her long, but he couldn't remember seeing her happy.

"No, I won't be meeting with them, nor do you need to let them know I'm here. You can leave now."

Brianna glared at Gwen, who had turned her attention back to the computer. Doug watched Brianna as she headed out the door. When she closed it behind her, Doug turned back to Gwen, whose glare seemed to melt slightly.

"That was fun," Doug said. "Now, what's our next step?"

Chapter 28

Brianna leaned against the door of Gwen's office, gulping air. Her heart raced. Seeing Doug hadn't elicited any pull whatsoever, but it confirmed her suspicions. The man at the casino who had asked Shelby about her was Doug. It was him all those times she felt like someone was watching her. And now he and Gwen were scheming together in her workplace.

Was he the reason the invoices and statements didn't match? Brianna had never understood his business deals, even though Doug always got away with things, including her money. But he usually worked with someone, a person with inside information. Gwen knew everything about Raeburn's business. She had access to all the bank accounts and control over which applicants got apartments. Brianna's eyes widened at the realization that Doug and Gwen were in on this together.

Voices drifted from the lobby down the hall. Brianna didn't have time to figure all this out now. Closing her eyes, she took a deep breath and stretched her neck from side to side. Sara and Jared would go ballistic if they knew Doug was here, and she wouldn't have a chance to figure out exactly what Doug and Gwen were up to. Doug would run if he were found out. She didn't know Gwen well enough to predict her reaction.

Brianna's best course of action was to pretend everything was fine. There was no reason she couldn't get through the rest of the afternoon. Then she would sit down and tell Raeburn what she knew. She owed him that much.

Calmer now that she had a plan, Brianna walked to the lobby. Jared and Sara sipped their water while Raeburn chatted about the benefits of the Women's Shelter and Support Agency his company supported. He stopped his monologue when he noticed Brianna.

"What took so long? I was ready to come look for you." Raeburn studied her, then asked, "Are you okay? You look like you've seen a ghost."

Aware that Sara was also watching her, Brianna shrugged. "I'm fine. Gwen called while I was looking for the keys." She swallowed hard. Sticking as close to the truth as she could, she added, "She had a few other things she wanted me to do."

Raeburn clapped his hands together. "We better get going. I'm happy to drive us all."

Brianna glanced at Sara and noticed the attorney studying her. She could make it through an apartment tour, but Brianna didn't know if she could keep up pretenses during the car ride.

Jared saved her from having to try. "We've got a rental car, Carl, and an appointment to get to afterward." Jared glanced at his watch. "Makes more sense for us to follow you, and we can leave from there."

"Works for me," said Raeburn. "Brianna, you can ride with me."

AT THE APARTMENT, Brianna tugged at the shoulder strap of her purse and sighed. Raeburn ended up leading the tour, giving her plenty of time to observe Sara and Jared. Nothing seemed out of the ordinary. Jared nodded along to Raeburn's commentary, as he had already seen what the Women's Shelter and Support Agency did. Sara, on the other hand, had lots of questions.

"Why did you go to this much trouble fixing up the apartments and then fitting them with such shabby accommodations?" Sara pointed to the pendant light over the kitchen counter. "They look used to me."

She'd been so worried about keeping tabs on Sara, Brianna hadn't noticed her surroundings. The sight forced her brows together. These weren't the same fixtures that were in the apartment the last time she was here. She slowly walked around the perimeter of the room and took a mental inventory. Sure enough, several other light fixtures had been swapped out and replaced with lower quality ones.

On a hunch, Brianna stepped into the bathroom and saw that the faucets weren't the ones she'd seen earlier, either. The handmade pottery toothbrush holder and hand soap dispenser no longer flanked the faucet. Instead, cheap plastic ones sat on the countertop.

She hustled through the other bathroom and bedrooms and discovered that all the items she'd selected for the new tenants had been replaced with flimsy substitutes. Shaking her head, she wondered how long it had been going on.

Brianna didn't have to guess who was behind it, but she didn't have proof. Even if she did, would Raeburn believe her? He didn't know Doug, but he did know and trust Gwen. After seeing her with Doug, Brianna suspected Gwen wasn't who she appeared to be either. She considered telling Raeburn now, but then Sara and Jared would find out Doug was here. And Sara might jump to the conclusion that Brianna and Doug were a couple again.

Brianna sighed. This was a chance to do the right thing and tell Raeburn about her suspicions. Her past was her past and she couldn't change that, but she could change how she acted in the present, and it wasn't going to do any good if she kept her suspicions to herself.

Walking back into the kitchen, Brianna said, "Mr. Raeburn, can I talk to you?"

Much to her chagrin, three sets of eyes focused on her.

"In a minute." Raeburn pulled out a red plastic plate with a crack in it and tapped it on the counter. "Can you tell me what happened to the nice bowls and dishes that were in here the last time I came through? I understand these women have kids, but that's no reason to provide them with subpar kitchenware."

"I don't know. None of this was here last time." Brianna scanned the countertops and pointed. "There used to be a cookie jar right there. It was in the shape of a dog. I picked it out myself because the lease doesn't allow pets and I thought it would be nice to have something in the house for the kids." She opened a cabinet above the sink and shook her head. "The cups are different too."

"What happened?" Sara asked.

Brianna opened the silverware drawer and her shoulders fell. The pieces she had picked out had squared-off handles that would have been easy for kids to use. What she saw in the drawer had rounded ends with molded flowers. She counted the spoons and shook her head. "Not only is this not the flatware I picked, but there're also only six settings. There should be twelve."

She ran her hand through her hair and looked at Sara. The lawyer made her feel uneasy, but if she continued to keep the facts to herself, she would incriminate herself. "Someone removed everything they thought was valuable and replaced it with cheap crap."

To prove her point, Brianna opened the door of the cabinet where the pots and pans were kept. She pulled one out, shaking her head. Instead of the brand-new, shiny, nonstick ones she'd ordered, the pan in her hand showed evidence of use: brown marks on the bottom, along with a few scratches on the side, and a chunk of missing plastic from the handle made it obvious.

Jared asked, "Has this happened before?"

"Never." Raeburn spoke up before Brianna could respond. "Gwen and Brianna know this isn't acceptable. We set up each apartment with roughly the same items. Everyone knows the drill."

Everyone but Doug, thought Brianna. *Was that why he was in Gwen's office? Would she risk her job for a loser like Doug Gerome?*

Sara cleared her throat, and Brianna looked up. The attorney studied her, and Brianna suspected what was going to happen next.

"Have you used any new vendors, Carl? What changes have you made lately?"

Brianna closed her eyes. She knew the only answer Raeburn could give. Might as well answer for him.

"I'm the newest member of the team, Ms. Shaw." She turned her gaze to Raeburn before she added, "I didn't do this. I followed protocol and have the documentation to prove it. I would never do anything to hurt this project. It's too important. Too many women don't have the support they need. Sure, we could purchase cheaper housewares for the apartments, but we didn't. *I* didn't."

A hand touched her shoulder, and she turned. Raeburn gave her a smile as he consoled her. "No one is accusing you of anything."

Sara shrugged. "Well, it looks suspicious to me. Just because Tasha forgave you doesn't mean I do." She pointed at the pan Brianna was still holding. "Although I never thought you'd sink to switching out pots and pans."

"Who's Tasha?" asked Raeburn.

Jared shook his head. "Sara, it's not relevant."

"What's not relevant?" Raeburn looked back and forth between Sara and Brianna. "What's going on here?"

Taking a deep breath, Brianna thought through her options. If she told the truth, Raeburn might keep her on. After all, she hadn't done anything wrong. If she lied, well, she knew what happened when people lied.

"I've met Ms. Shaw and Mr. Hughes before," she confessed.

"That part I figured out. What I don't understand is why Sara thinks you have something to do with this."

"I don't know if she had anything to do with it," said Sara, "but some people aren't what they seem."

"You're referring to Doug, not me."

"Who's Doug?" asked Raeburn.

Jared glanced at his watch. "If we're going to make our appointment, we need to wrap this up. Shall we let Brianna explain what's going on? It might be faster that way."

Sara shrugged. "Fine. But I reserve the right to add any relevant information."

Brianna gave Jared a half smile before she addressed Raeburn. "I was a temp in Ms. Shaw's previous office."

Mr. Raeburn nodded but frowned. "Okay. . . ."

"I also dated Ms. Shaw's brother-in-law." Brianna paused. She didn't want Raeburn to think badly of her, and she needed to phrase this right. Before she had a chance, though, Sara spoke.

"While he was married to my sister. I'm sorry to have to bring that up, but your latest employee isn't the most trustworthy."

Brianna threw her hands in the air. "For the millionth time, Doug never mentioned he was married. By the time I found out, the damage was done. Trust me, if I knew what he was really like, I never would have gotten involved with him. My judgement in men is horrible, but I would never steal, particularly from women and children in need. I had nothing to do with what happened here."

She looked from Raeburn's face to Sara's, then Jared's. Brianna didn't care what Sara or Jared thought, but if her new boss believed them, then it was pointless to argue. Maybe she was a bad judge of character, even of those who were supposed to be on her side.

"As interesting as that situation sounds, can we focus on who else has access to these keys? That will tell us who might have changed the apartment," Raeburn said.

The answer wasn't going to help her, but Brianna knew she had to respond. "The keys are kept in Gwen's office, locked in her drawer. Gwen is the only one who—" Brianna stopped mid-sentence. Now was the time to come clean. Doug had been in Gwen's office an hour ago. The question was, Would Sara and Jared believe her, or was the damage done? She should have told them as soon as she knew Doug was involved, but now she didn't have a choice.

Before she could mention her suspicion, though, Raeburn asked, "You think Gwen had something to do with this? That's crazy. She's been with me for years and nothing like this has ever happened before. There has to be someone else."

Brianna moistened her lips. The only way to save herself was to confess to Doug being in the office, but Gwen seemed adamant that Doug's presence be kept a secret. Once again, she found herself between a rock and a hard place.

Knowing she had to take care of herself since no one else would, she focused on Raeburn. "The keys are kept locked in one of Gwen's desk drawers. She and I are the only two with access." She held up a hand toward Sara. "Someone could have stolen the keys, but Gwen would have noticed. And even though I've had ample opportunity to make copies, I didn't do it. You are welcome to search my purse and desk at the office."

Sara laughed. "You're smarter than that. You'd put them someplace we'd never think to look."

Jared placed his hand on Sara's shoulder. "Setting aside your history, I think Brianna is telling the truth."

Brianna wondered if the expression on her own face resembled the shocked one on Sara's. She didn't get to find out, though, because she forced herself to continue speaking.

"There is something else you need to know." She steeled herself for the backlash she expected before she continued. "Doug . . . was sitting in Gwen's office when I went in to get the key. The two of them were having some sort of meeting. It's possible he has something to do with this."

"Gwen's out sick today. How could she have a meeting?" Raeburn paused as the pieces of the puzzle started to fit together. "Is this the same Doug you dated? Sara's brother-in-law? Why would he be talking to Gwen?"

"*Ex*-brother-in-law. That's what he does. That man is always trying to make an easy dollar," Sara said as she threw up her hands. "Why didn't you mention he was here? You know as well as I do how manipulative he is. He might have convinced Gwen to help him. Or Cynthia. She'd love a chance to create controversy."

Raeburn sat down on the kitchen barstool. "Hold on. That name sounds familiar. Who is Cynthia?"

Jared cleared his throat. "She's a local journalist who contacted Sara about your project. I believe she already interviewed you."

"Oh yes. I remember her. She asked great questions," Raeburn said, then frowned. "Why would she have anything to do with what's happened here?"

Brianna, Jared, and Sara looked at each other. Sara shook her head and sat down next to Raeburn. "If I explain it, I'll get more upset."

Jared gestured to Brianna.

She chewed on her lip, trying to figure out where to start. The silence got heavy the longer she waited.

Finally, Jared stepped in. "Cynthia and Sara grew up in

the same town. From what I gather, they didn't always get along. When Doug showed up in Glen Valley last year, he stirred up some trouble for our riverfront restoration. Cynthia wrote a less-than-complimentary article about Sara—"

Sara interrupted, "Which was erroneous and eventually retracted."

Jared nodded. "Yes, but not before the town showed up in full force at Sara's office to protest."

Brianna would have given anything to see that, but she kept that thought to herself. Now that everyone was on the same page, she needed to share the rest of her suspicions about Doug. Before she could open her mouth, Jared glanced at his watch again.

"We need to leave if we're going to make our appointment."

Sara started to protest, but something in Jared's look silenced her. Something about the wordless argument told Brianna they weren't disagreeing over work. This was personal. Neither Sara nor Jared spoke, but when Sara turned to Raeburn, Brianna knew Jared had won whatever argument they were having.

"I'm sorry. We can't be late."

Brianna watched as Sara extracted a promise from Raeburn to keep her updated on the situation. They shook hands, then Sara turned to Brianna. Brianna braced herself. Sara had every right to criticize her—for what she did today and what she had done in the past.

Rather than lashing out, Sara shook her head. "Don't let Doug get to you. We both know you're better than that."

When the door closed behind them, Raeburn turned and stared at her. "Okay. How about you go over this with me again? It's going to take me a while to digest it all."

Chapter 29

Once Brianna had updated Raeburn on his company's accounting issues and her sordid history with Doug, they contacted the police. She spent the next few hours going over all the items in the apartment that were missing. Brianna pulled up the inventory of the furnishings on her cell phone and knew the receipts were in her apartment. The differences between the statements and receipts made sense now. Raeburn agreed with the detective: Brianna had discovered how Gwen had used the furnishing purchases to make fake returns, stealing a large amount of money from the Women's Shelter and Support Agency.

When Brianna mentioned the plumbing and window treatment vendors, Raeburn held up a hand. "Those companies aren't on my list of preferred vendors."

"My guess is they're fake companies," the detective offered. "Your Miss Martin probably set them up and paid herself. At least Miss Thompson tracked it. You'd never believe how many people don't know what's been stolen. I get calls weeks and months post-crime because the items weren't noticed." He looked at the list Brianna had made and smiled. "This makes my job easier."

She resisted smiling back. The detective might think things were easy, but Brianna knew how slippery Doug could be. And it was only a guess as to how Gwen was involved. Raeburn rescued her from having to respond.

"What's your next step?"

The detective snapped his notebook closed and put it in his pocket. "We'll keep an eye out for items matching the descriptions in pawn shops and online exchanges. Most of this stuff is easy to dispose of, which is what makes the scheme a moneymaker for whoever's behind it. If this has been going on for a while, you may have lost tens of thousands of dollars in the last few months. We can investigate the vendors you questioned as well. If they are covers, it'll be obvious."

Raeburn let out a long sigh and closed his eyes.

Brianna immediately felt guilty. "I'm sorry." She couldn't help thinking she should have figured out what was happening before today.

He shook his head. "I put you in a horrible position. If I'd paid more attention to what was going on, I would have noticed something sooner."

"This isn't your fault, Mr. Raeburn. Even with this newest twist, this job is better than the one I had with Alex." Her statement was more or less truthful. Alex might have been a pain to work for, but he hadn't made her an accessory to a crime. At least not that she was aware of.

"Still, someone I trusted stole from me." He opened his eyes and smiled at Brianna. "This isn't what I expected of Gwen."

"It might not be Gwen. Doug has a history of getting people to do things they don't want to do."

"What is it he made *you* do?"

She'd been dreading the question, but Brianna knew it would come up sooner or later. The only thing she could do now was tell the truth. It was up to Raeburn to decide if she was still worthy of a job or not.

"Doug used my experience in real estate to buy some properties far below their value."

Raeburn pursed his lips. "You negotiated a better price for your client. That's what agents do."

Nodding, she said, "Yes, but the data points Doug wanted me to use weren't relevant." She took a deep breath to steady herself before she told the story. "Doug found out about some developers who wanted to work in Saint Thomas. He asked me to help him put together a proposal for all the individual landowners the developers planned to approach. He never told me how he got the information, but Doug knew exactly what properties were needed and how much the developers were willing to pay.

"I didn't know what was going on, but the property Doug targeted resold at a premium. I didn't take any more time to research it or I would have known he was extorting money."

Raeburn said, "Doug bought the land for less than market value and then resold it to the development group for a profit. That sounds like good business practice."

She shook her head. "My boss didn't think so. Especially after it came out that my personal money had been used in the process. Money I never got back. It looked like I was the one who had orchestrated the sales. I was asked to leave to prevent a criminal investigation."

"This isn't a coincidence that Doug followed you to Vegas, is it?"

"I don't know. I followed him to Glen Valley, which is how I met Sara and Jared."

"This is beginning to sound like a reality TV show," said the detective. "But I have to ask, why would you follow the guy?"

Brianna admonished herself for forgetting the police were listening to everything she said.

"Doug used $100,000 of my money. He promised he'd give it back, but he never did. That was my life savings, which would have been easy to replenish if I'd kept my job. But I left. It was too embarrassing to face the truth—I'd fallen for a bad guy. And everyone on the island turned against me." She shook her head. "I don't blame them, really. I've always had bad taste in men, but it didn't usually involve extortion."

The detective looked at his notepad. "You said you met the attorneys in Glen Valley. Did they know this Doug, too?"

She'd already explained this to Raeburn but repeated it for the detective's benefit. Brianna hoped Raeburn wouldn't change his mind when he heard the story again. If he fired her, she would have to start over. Again. She sighed, knowing this was all her fault anyway.

"I was dating Doug while he was still Sara's brother-in-law." The detective's eyes got big, but she continued, "Jared hired Doug to run a renovation project in Glen Valley. Doug didn't last long before he was fired. I knew of Sara before I went to Glen Valley and ended up working as a temporary receptionist in her law office for the day. Once she realized who I was, she let me go. But not before Doug showed up and got into an argument with Jared."

"Which is why he got fired," finished Raeburn. "I think I'm beginning to understand a little about this man."

"I can reach out to the police department in Glen Valley and see if there's anything outstanding we can use to bring in Doug Gerome," the detective said. "If we have him out of the way, you can work on figuring out how your other employee is involved."

"Maybe she isn't, Mr. Raeburn. Doug might have used her like he used me. Gwen could be an innocent party to all this."

Her boss nodded, but Brianna thought he looked skeptical, which meant when this was all over she would be in search of a new job. Par for the course. But at least this time she planned to follow through with straightening out the problem.

"What else can I do for you?" Brianna asked.

"I've got all I need for now," the detective said, and he handed each of them his business card. "If anything comes up, call me. I'll give you updates as they arise."

The detective showed himself out, and Brianna watched Raeburn as he sat on the couch.

"I wasn't expecting this."

She followed him to the couch. Instead of sitting, she leaned against the arm. Before she could speak, he said, "I know you didn't have anything to do with this."

"But you don't know me." Brianna didn't want to cause herself more problems, but she had to be honest. "We both know Alex isn't much of a reference."

She bit her lip when she heard Raeburn's laugh.

"No, but when he lies, it's easy to tell. He talked about what great work you did all the time. I've seen it for myself the last month or so."

"Then you won't mind me saying something else about Gwen?" She should have told the detective, but for some reason, she had a sense of loyalty to Raeburn. "Well, two things, actually."

He nodded for her to continue.

"I'm not sure if you've noticed Gwen's choice of footwear. . . ."

He shrugged. "She wears high heels that make a lot of noise when she walks."

"They're also designer—at least four hundred dollars a pair. I noticed she never wears the same pair twice, and she always shops over the lunch hour." Brianna hesitated. Gwen might be getting the shoes on sale for all she knew, but it made more sense that she was pocketing the money from Raeburn's Women's Shelter and Support Agency to pay for her shopping sprees. "It's none of my business, but I'm guessing her salary doesn't cover the cost of that many high-end shoes."

Raeburn nodded. "It *isn't* any of your business, but I see your point. What else?"

Brianna told him about the client, Lorraine, and how she had ended up with one of the apartments despite being gainfully employed.

He listened, asking a few questions, shaking his head when he got answers that bothered him. "There is no reason someone like that should be living in one of our apartments. She isn't in crisis. She didn't meet the basic parameters I set up for the facilities."

Nodding her agreement, Brianna continued, "Gwen shut me down when I pushed back on Lorraine. She had a lot of reasons why Suzanne, the other woman, didn't qualify and would make a bad resident."

"Tell me."

"Suzanne is unemployed with five kids, has a restraining order against her ex, and didn't interview well. Gwen said the boys were too destructive to get an apartment, even though the family is living out of a car that's in the process of being repossessed."

Raeburn grimaced. Brianna was glad his irritation wasn't directed at her. "That is the *perfect* person for our apartments. We can help normalize her life while she gets back on her feet. She's the reason I set up the center in the first place." Shaking his head, he said, "I need to get to the bottom of this. But for now, let's go home and get some rest. We can tackle this tomorrow." He stood up and held out his hand. "Thank you, Brianna, for being honest and helping me with this."

She shook his outstretched hand, feeling for the first time in a long time that she had some value to give.

Chapter 30

"I can't believe China is involved with all this." Sara tossed the hotel key card on the credenza and dropped her briefcase and suitcase next to it. "And Doug. That man never goes away, does he?"

"Her name is Brianna. And, yes, Doug is like a cockroach. Nothing short of a nuclear explosion keeps him down," said Jared as he looked at the paper in his hands. "We got to the courthouse just in time. Another thirty minutes and we would have missed the appointment."

Sara threw herself down on the king-size bed. "I need a drink after that mess." She patted the space next to her. "Can we relax before dinner? The restaurant could hold the reservation, couldn't they?"

She smiled as Jared lay down, covering her body with his. His warm lips skimmed over hers. Sara's muscles relaxed and her eyes closed as she prepared to enjoy Jared's touch, but they shot open again when she felt herself being lifted off the bed.

"Do you know how long it took me to get this reservation? Three months. And no, they don't hold reservations. Late won't work." He took hold of her shoulders and lifted her up, then guided her to the bathroom. "Besides, we should celebrate. Get ready!"

After grabbing a change of clothes and her toiletries, Sara let herself into the bathroom and closed the door behind her. She draped her clothes over the stool, put her makeup bag on the counter, and looked at herself in the mirror. Her flushed cheeks and swollen lips needed to return to normal before she and Jared left for dinner.

Since she didn't have time to redo her hair and makeup, she tucked her hair under a shower cap and entered the shower, careful to keep the water off her face. The hot water washed over her as she considered what she should do next.

Brianna wasn't as bad as she'd originally thought, but someone had stolen from their project. It wouldn't happen again. As she rinsed the soapsuds off her body, Sara debated how much Doug had to do with the situation. If today was the first time he'd been to town, Doug couldn't be the one pilfering items. But she knew Doug was capable of clandestine operations. Case in point: cheating on his wife.

But there was also Gwen Martin. Sara hadn't met her, but something felt off about her. Why call in sick and then sneak into the office to meet with someone? If everything was above board, this behavior seemed suspicious.

Turning off the water, Sara toweled off with the fluffy towel, making a mental note to mention to the front desk that the towels left lint everywhere.

Sara applied her body lotion and tied the wrap dress around her waist. She freshened up her makeup before pulling off her shower cap, letting her brunette hair fall to her shoulders. If she were into the mussy look, she would leave it as is, but she liked things sleek and straight. A few minutes combing out her hair and a copious amount of hairspray and she was out of the bathroom.

"I'm ready. Do you need to use the—"

Whatever she had planned to say next vanished as she took in the transformed hotel room. In the time she'd showered and preened, someone had arranged candles and bouquets of flowers throughout the room. The candles sparkled in the dim lighting, and Sara smiled as the scent of roses hit her. A silver champagne bucket sat on the coffee table, where white rose petals had been scattered.

Sara held her breath as she watched Jared step toward her. He reached out, and she gave him her hand. Jared pulled her close, giving her a soft kiss on the mouth.

"Surprise!"

As much as she wanted to stay with Jared and enjoy the room, Sara pushed away from him. "Don't we have a dinner reservation waiting for us?"

Jared led her to the couch, where he sat, pulling her down next to him. He took the bottle of champagne out of the bucket and dried it with the towel.

"I have a confession." He popped the cork from the bottle. "There is no reservation, although dinner will be delivered in an hour."

Sara wondered if her face reflected her shock. "You had this planned all along? This is supposed to be a celebratory event. Don't you want to take me out?"

Jared shook his head as he poured each of them a glass of wine. "I do. But how often do we get a chance to enjoy a romantic night in?" He handed her a champagne flute.

"What if I wanted to go out?"

Jared winked back at her. "I have other things planned for this evening." He raised his glass. "To us."

A grin plastered itself on Sara's face. A soft clink sounded when she touched Jared's glass. "To us."

They each took a sip, and Sara snuggled into Jared's shoulder. He shifted, and the flute disappeared from her hand. Jared's hand tilted her head toward his and she felt his smooth lips brush over hers. She took his bottom lip and bit down gently. The smile on Jared's face told her what she needed to know.

Sara stood up and said, "Let's get to your plan, then," and pulled the tie on her dress.

Chapter 31

Brianna closed the door to her apartment and dropped her stuff on the floor. What a day.

Gwen had lied to her. Doug showed up out of the blue. Raeburn questioned her loyalty. She didn't want to know what Sara and Jared thought about her. If she was lucky, she would still have a job tomorrow.

"Why do I have such bad luck?" she muttered to herself.

Her stomach rumbled, and she did a mental inventory of what she had stashed in the kitchen. Ramen noodles were her best bet for the evening. With a sigh, she headed toward the kitchen.

She pulled out one of Kevin's pans, filled it at the faucet, and placed it on the stovetop. Then she turned the burner on high and headed back to her room to change.

No sense watching the water boil, she thought as she unbuttoned her shirt. That was a bonus of Naomi being gone. She could undress whenever and wherever she wanted.

The shirt slid off her shoulders as she entered her bedroom. Brianna tossed it toward the pile of dirty clothes in the corner. She rummaged through the clean laundry she'd dumped on the floor on the other side of the room to find a pair of pajamas. She didn't want Rosemary to take her clothes by mistake again, but she wouldn't mind having them magically washed, pressed, and folded, either.

"This is a better show than the one I left at the casino."

She grabbed the first shirt she touched and clutched it to her chest as she whirled around to face her ex-boyfriend. Leaning against the wall with his hands tucked into the pockets of his jeans, Doug acted like he was standing in his own bedroom.

"How did you get in here?" Brianna's heart pounded in her chest. "Breaking and entering is against the law."

With a smirk on his face, Doug pushed himself off the wall. "I like what you've done with the place. Minimalism suits you."

He took a step toward her, and she moved closer to the door.

"What do you want?"

"Obviously not money. You don't have any. Or furniture. Or clothes."

Brianna knew Doug was right and nothing in her apartment was worth anything, but she also knew he should not be here.

"Turn around." She twirled her index finger in the air.

Doug laughed and asked, "Why? I've seen you naked before."

Brianna shook her head. "That was the past. Turn around or get out. Your choice. My preference is for you to leave."

She knew he wouldn't leave until he was ready, and there was nothing she could do to make him turn around, but something about her request got to Doug. He walked to the window and stared out. When his back was turned, Brianna pulled the T-shirt over her head.

"What do you want?" she asked as she rubbed at the wrinkles in the shirt. She frowned when the first place Doug looked was at her chest. "Seriously? If you needed to check out a set of boobs, you could go anywhere in the city."

He shook his head. "Is that a new shirt? I don't remember it."

She glanced down to check what she was wearing and grimaced when she saw what she'd grabbed. A unicorn with a rainbow horn spouting out sparkling confetti proclaimed, *Everything is better with a unicorn.* It wasn't the sentiment she wanted to convey right now, but she didn't plan to change to suit the situation.

"It was cute and I'm a sucker for unicorns," she spat out. A quick glance around the bedroom reminded her she'd left her cell phone in the kitchen, along with the water on the stove. That gave her the perfect excuse to leave the room. "I'm making dinner. Feel free to let yourself out."

Without waiting for his response, Brianna dashed through the door and hurried to the kitchen. She grabbed her phone, ready to dial 911. Doug hadn't been violent before, but after hearing some of the stories from the applicants at work, she wasn't taking any chances. Especially since she knew he was working with her boss.

"You didn't answer my question," she said when she heard footsteps enter the kitchen. Brianna forced herself to stay calm, checking the water before turning to face Doug. She crossed her arms over her chest, keeping the phone ready. "I assume Gwen gave you my address? Or have you added stalker to your résumé?"

Doug leaned against the doorjamb, assuming his standard devil-may-care attitude. His relaxed posture and disheveled hair attracted her when they'd first met. It might have worked if he'd been nicer to her when they ran into each other in Glen Valley. But that was then. Standing in her kitchen, she felt nothing. Somewhere between Glen Valley and Las Vegas, Doug had lost his charm.

"How have you been?" he asked. Instead of waiting for an

answer, he pointed at her plant. Brianna gasped when she saw Philomena was dead. "Still can't keep a plant alive, either. Should've stopped trying. You suck at it."

Sadness overwhelmed her when she thought of how disappointed Rosemary would be. She should've given the girl the plant when she'd asked for it instead of being selfish.

Ignoring him, she dumped the noodles into the boiling water. She stirred them, then got a bowl from the cabinet. Brianna set it down on the counter harder than usual, in hopes he would get the hint that he wasn't welcome.

When he stood there looking at her, she asked, "How did you get in here?"

"I picked the lock. Which was hard even with the correct tools. You need to have a locksmith look at it."

"No kidding." She waved her arms around the room. "I need a lot of things, but some of us don't have money for general household repairs."

She turned back to the stove, the noodles forgotten. A few months ago, she would have welcomed Doug back into her life even though he had stolen her money and ruined her reputation. But seeing him today with Gwen, she didn't care. She was over him after all. Who needed a man who ignored the consequences of his actions?

"Aren't you going to ask me how I've been?"

Her eyebrow raised as she said, "I'd rather you got out of my apartment so I can eat my dinner in peace. Or I can call the police."

"No need to call the police. Go ahead. Eat. I'm not stopping you." He tucked his hands into his pockets and glanced sideways at her.

She recognized his change in tactics. The expression on his face resembled a sad puppy dog waiting for attention. But his time it wasn't going to work. At least that's what she told herself until Doug spoke again.

"I want to get back together."

Chapter 32

Brianna's body went rigid, and the only sound in the room was the noise of the water bubbling in the pan. Doug stared at her face. He watched it change as she processed what he said. Anger pulled her eyebrows down into points. Sadness brought a tear to her eye. Need flushed her cheeks.

That response told him he might have a chance after all. He'd ruined his marriage and probably lost his children's love, but maybe Brianna would take him back. All he had to do was explain what he was doing with Gwen.

He moved forward, and she backed closer to the stove. Doug hesitated, then stepped back.

"I'm not going to hurt you."

Brianna ripped open the seasoning packet and poured it into the pot. She stirred it as she spoke. "I know. I'm finished letting you or anyone else get to me. My ability to judge people's character has improved since the last time you saw me."

The admission startled him. Brianna had always been an easy target. When they first got together, he'd used her naivety for his own purposes. He used everyone, but it was easier when someone was as easily manipulated as her.

But she was different now. He had noticed it when she walked into Gwen's office earlier that day. She didn't seem to have any feelings for him. No smile. No flip of the hair. Their interaction was sterile.

That could be changed, though. He'd make her see over dinner that they were still good for each other.

"Do I get a bowl of those noodles?" he asked. "I haven't had a chance to eat all day."

He jerked in surprise when Brianna turned toward him with a grimace. "No. You do not get dinner. I can barely afford to feed myself, and the last time I checked, breaking and entering does not include a dinner invitation. Get out."

The tone of her voice startled him. She sounded like she really didn't want him here. But she had always wanted him. That's what had allowed him to borrow her money. She loved him and couldn't say no.

"You don't mean that."

"Why not? It's not like there's anything between us anymore."

"There was."

"Past tense. If I hadn't learned my lesson in Saint Thomas and Glen Valley, you've made it loud and clear here in Vegas."

Doug frowned. He could see why she would still be mad about the past, but nothing had happened yet in Vegas. He'd been so busy with the job for Gwen, he hadn't had time to reach out to Brianna. It was only because she'd seen him in Gwen's office that he decided to stop by tonight and see how she was. Was that why she was mad at him? He hadn't come to visit her soon enough?

"I haven't seen you since I got here, other than today in Gwen's office. And at the casino." He didn't admit he'd been following her that day. She wouldn't like that. "I've missed you though."

Brianna turned off the burner and poured the noodles and broth into the bowl. Without a word, she picked up her spoon and slurped the soup. He hated it when she made noise like that, and she knew it. He also knew if he complained, Brianna would continue.

Two could play at this game.

"What do you do for Gwen?" he asked. He already knew, but Brianna wasn't reacting like he had thought she would.

The spoon paused halfway to her mouth. "Don't be stupid. You and Gwen used me. Go bother her."

The last thing he wanted to do was spend more time with that woman. Instead, Doug turned to the sparsely furnished living room.

"I didn't think you liked this look." He wandered around the room. "Why the hell do you have a laundry basket in your living room? This doesn't look comfortable at all."

"My former roommate stole all my stuff. Like you stole my money. Apparently I never learn."

Surprised by her explanation, he lowered himself onto a chair and tapped his knuckles on the table. "And you decided to replace your things with this secondhand crap?"

Shaking her head, Brianna said, "My neighbor and his daughter found that for me. They helped me when I was down. Instead of kicking me."

His gut twisted. "*He* found it? How nice of *him*. Sleeping with all the dads in the building, are ya?"

His comment backfired when Brianna threw back her head and laughed. It wasn't the cheerful sound he loved. This cackle reminded him of a villain from the animated movies his ex-wife had forced him to watch with his son and daughter. The mean old woman who stole the Dalmatian puppies popped into his head for a moment but disappeared when Brianna spoke.

"You don't get to be jealous of anything I do anymore, Doug. We're long past that. If anyone should be mad right now, it's me. Once again you've put my job on the line with your stupid business schemes."

Doug shrugged. "I don't know what you're talking about. Gwen and I have an arrangement that doesn't include you."

"That's crap and you know it."

Brianna tossed the bowl of noodles into the sink, and he smirked when he heard pottery shatter. He'd gotten under her skin, and it felt great. The calm and collected Brianna didn't turn him on, but the passionate one? This made showing up in her apartment worth it.

"She's using you," Brianna said pointedly.

The statement caught him off guard. After today's meeting, Doug had suspected Gwen might be up to something, and Brianna's comment fueled his doubt.

Holding up his hands, Doug said, "All I'm doing is moving stuff out of apartments into a storage unit."

"What happens to the stuff in the storage unit?"

He'd learned in this business not to ask too many questions. That way he could legitimately say he didn't know. Gwen didn't offer any details, and he didn't want to know.

But he knew someone else was disposing of the items he put in the first storage unit, and the products he put back in the apartments weren't worth nearly as much as those he took. His head throbbed as he realized his mistake. Gwen was making a boatload of money and paying him a token amount for his troubles. She was probably laughing behind his back right now.

Doug ground his teeth together. Leaning back in the chair, he considered his options. He didn't want trouble. Just some easy money and a woman. Brianna used to be both those things. The job with Gwen had been promising, but he had no desire to be her patsy.

Doug pushed back his chair. "I'm outta here. This ain't worth my time. There're better things to do in this town, and I'm not getting caught in this mess." He stomped to the door, his stomach rumbling on the way. "You know, you could've had me back. But don't bother now."

Doug tried to open the door, but it stuck. He shook it a few times, but nothing worked. His dramatic exit had failed.

Turning back to Brianna, he said, "Get me out of here. It ain't safe to be in this hellhole."

He gave the handle one more pull and the door flew open, hitting him in the shoulder. Doug heard Brianna laugh, but he marched out the door and slammed it behind him. The night was still young. He could find a woman to get him dinner.

Chapter 33

As soon as the door slammed shut, Brianna's laughter stopped. She raced over and slid the security chain into place. She was safe. For now, anyway.

A random thought popped into her head: *What if Doug blackmailed Mr. Raeburn?* She wouldn't put it past him to ask her boss for money in exchange for information about what Gwen was doing. Or go as far as to lie and say Brianna was the one at fault.

"Calm down," she mumbled to herself. "You're over-reacting."

Doug might not care if what he did was legal or moral, but he wasn't stupid. If he approached Raeburn, he'd implicate himself. No, hopefully he was gone for good.

If only she were that lucky.

But she knew luck wasn't going to get her out of the mess with the statements and receipts at the office. She still didn't have proof, but Gwen had to be behind the phone calls, canceling the furniture orders. It made sense to hire someone new and let them take the fall.

It was obvious now she thought about it. Gwen had taught her everything about the job. It would be easy for Gwen to alter things to make it look like Brianna had canceled the orders and pocketed the money. At least Brianna hadn't paid the fake vendors Gwen set up.

Even though Brianna could prove the cancellations, she didn't know where to find the missing cash. Without that proof, she had nothing.

Her eyes burned as she fought back tears. Once again, she'd been duped into something. She wasn't the type of person to have an affair with a married man, and she didn't believe stealing money from companies was the right thing to do, either.

What she was, though, was a gullible woman who thought other people could fix her life. And once again, that fix was going to make her look like the bad guy. If only she'd focused more on getting her real estate license back, she wouldn't be in this position.

"This sucks!" she yelled to the empty apartment. "Why can't anything go right in my life?" She considered beating the floor with her fists, but she knew the lady in 3B might call and complain. Then she'd probably be kicked out of her apartment, too. Wouldn't that be the icing on the cake?

Frustrated by the futility of the situation, Brianna shuffled to the kitchen to clean up the mess she'd made. She picked the pieces of the broken bowl out of the sink. As she tossed the shards into the trash, she chastised herself for losing her temper. It hadn't done any good, and it had cost her a bowl.

Losing control never did anything good for her. Every time she let her emotions get the best of her, she ended up making the wrong decision.

Brianna mentally listed all the mistakes she'd made when she felt a sharp stab in her index finger. She looked down to see a sliver of the bowl sticking out of her hand.

"Of course. Everything bad happens to me. Why do I bother?"

She plucked the shard of pottery from her finger and

turned on the faucet. Red-tinged water flowed into the sink. She watched it circle down the drain, sort of like her life.

Her life wasn't going anywhere. Everything she tried ended up being another dead end. Vegas had been a gamble. She thought coming here would be her golden ticket. But there was no such thing as a golden ticket, at least not in the real world.

"If that's the case, why am I sticking around?"

She turned off the water and wrapped a paper towel around her finger before she reached under the sink and pulled out a trash bag. Before she could change her mind, she walked back to her bedroom and shoved her clean clothes in the bag. She started to toss in the dirties as well, but common sense stopped her. If she were leaving town, she didn't know when she'd be able to do laundry again. Best to keep things separate.

It only took a few minutes to pack everything she needed. She debated putting the puzzle into her bag. It reminded her of Rosemary and how the girl had overcome much bigger obstacles than Brianna ever would. But it also made her feel pathetic. How could a twelve-year-old deal with life and death while Brianna ran away at the first sign of trouble?

The sound of Shelby's ringtone distracted her from her wallowing. Brianna thought about ignoring the call, but if she was leaving town, she might as well say goodbye. She punched the answer button with her injured finger and winced.

"Stupid," she said before she answered. "Hello?"

"That's not the greeting I was expecting. What's wrong with you?"

Brianna shook her head. "Sorry. I was talking to myself." Blood seeped out of the paper towel, and Brianna headed back to the kitchen for reinforcements. "Glad you called."

"Are you dressed? Because I got free passes to the high rollers' room. Thought we could enjoy the free drinks and watch people lose money."

"As much as I want to, I'm actually on my way out of town."

"Why? Do you have a work trip?"

Pressing her temples, Brianna wished she had thought through her explanation better before she blurted it out. "Not exactly." She paused, not wanting to lie. Shelby deserved the truth. "I'm getting out of the city for a while. Work isn't going the way I planned. Better to leave now than to be asked to leave, if you know what I mean."

"Does this have something to do with the money that's missing?"

Brianna froze. She had forgotten she told Shelby about that.

"From your silence, I assume I'm right. So, let me ask you this: Isn't it going to look suspicious if you take off?"

"Yes, but—"

"No buts. If you leave, it will be harder to fix the problem. You've done the work and you know how much money is gone and who the likely suspect is. Why are you second-guessing yourself?"

Brianna ran her hand through her hair. "Because I'm a horrible judge of character, and if I'm wrong, Gwen will crucify me."

"And if you're right, you save Mr. Raeburn's project as well as the homes of several mothers and their children. Trust yourself. For once."

"It doesn't usually work out for me."

"Brianna, listen to me. This isn't a gamble. This is your life, and it's coming together. Don't make a rash decision you'll regret."

Even though she knew Shelby was right, she couldn't bring herself to admit it. Losing at so many aspects of life had left her feeling helpless. Leaving now was the only way to save what little dignity she had left.

"I'll call you when I get settled," she croaked. Brianna

swallowed the lump in her throat before she added, "Thank you for being there for me."

Shelby didn't sound happy, but she said, "I'm here if you need me."

Brianna hung up the phone and wiped the tears from her face. It hurt to leave her friend behind. Before she could change her mind, she finished packing. Then she checked the bus schedule to see where she could go. Seattle was the first bus out in the morning. She'd be trading the heat of the desert for the rain of the northwest.

Wondering if she should buy a raincoat on the way, Brianna set her alarm for 5:00 a.m. and headed to bed. She needed to be fresh for her escape the next morning. She was crawling under the covers when she heard the knock at the door. Frowning, Brianna debated who it could be. Doug wouldn't bother coming back. Shelby had probably decided to come over to nag her to stay.

She walked back to the door and took a deep breath. The faster she convinced Shelby she was making the right decision, the sooner she could go to bed.

Taking a deep breath, she flung open the door and said, "I'm not staying."

Kevin cocked his head. "I didn't know you were leaving."

Chapter 34

Brianna didn't know whether to be embarrassed or thrilled to see Kevin. Her gaze went to the floor, and she caught sight of her unicorn T-shirt. She chose embarrassment and crossed her arms over her chest, which put the paper towel on display.

"Do you always carry a paper towel around with you?" Kevin asked.

She unwrapped her finger and showed him the dried blood. "Cooking accident."

"Happens to the best of us." Kevin nodded. "Rosemary has a shirt like that."

She grinned. "I know. She told me about it, and I got one for myself." She looked down the hallway. "Where is she?"

"In bed. It's late for her and she has school tomorrow." He nodded toward her apartment. "I know it's late, but can I come in for a minute? I wanted to talk to you about something."

As much as she didn't want to deal with any other emotions tonight, she didn't want to turn Kevin away. This might be her last conversation with him. "What's up?" she asked as she gestured for him to come in.

Kevin opened his mouth to speak, but his eyes grew big.

"What's with the trash bags? Intense round of downsizing? Not that you have much to tidy," he joked. "Did you get that book about life-changing cleaning?"

"Tidying, not cleaning," Brianna corrected him, then paused. Now was her chance. They hadn't known each other long enough for Kevin to care one way or another. She might as well rip off the bandage. "Actually, I'm leaving. Naomi stole my suitcase, so I'm using trash bags instead."

She paused to look at Kevin's face and noticed he looked paler than he had when he walked in the door.

"Leaving? As in moving?"

"Yep. I thought I'd try my luck in Seattle."

Kevin walked to the kitchen table and sat down. "Do you mind if I ask why?"

Again, she forced herself to tell the truth. "I'm going to get fired tomorrow. I thought I'd make it easy on my boss."

"How do you know?"

"Do you remember the receipts and statements I was working on the other day?"

"The ones I offered to help you figure out?"

Guilt crept up her neck and she felt her face flush. "Yeah. Those would be the ones."

"If I help you figure them out, could you convince your boss not to fire you?"

For the first time since they sat down, Brianna studied Kevin's face. "Are you okay?" she asked.

"Not really. I came down to tell you about something Rosemary said." He put his head between his knees. "Give me a minute."

"Is *she* okay?"

Kevin nodded.

It didn't make sense. If everything was okay, why would he be here this late at night? It also didn't explain why he was about to pass out.

"Do you want some water?"

"Yes," he whispered.

She hesitated. What if Kevin passed out while she was in the kitchen? Even though it was only ten feet from here, she wouldn't be able to get back fast enough to catch him if he fell off the chair.

"Dramatic much?" she mumbled to herself, and she hurried to the kitchen. She filled a plastic cup as fast as she could. By the time she made it back to Kevin, his color was back to normal.

"Here. I didn't know if you wanted ice. I can get you some if you want."

"No. This works." He sipped the water and put it down on the table. "Sorry. You surprised me with your announcement."

She sat down next to Kevin and nodded. "Yeah. It's kind of a spur-of-the-moment decision."

"Were you going to tell us goodbye?"

Kevin's tone made her meet his eyes. The ice-blue color brought back the memory of the first time they'd met. He was holding a laundry basket of her perfectly folded clothes. It felt like ages ago, but she knew it had only been a month.

She hadn't planned to say goodbye. Running was easier. There was less chance of someone talking her out of leaving. She had made it through Shelby's phone call, but she didn't want to hurt anyone else, especially Kevin and his daughter.

When she opened her mouth to speak, her voice broke. "No. I didn't want to hurt Rosemary. She's gone through enough as it is."

He nodded and looked around the room. She watched his examination of the apartment and noticed when his gaze stopped on Philomena. "She'll be more hurt that you didn't stop by." He took a deep breath and started to stand up. "I should go. You have things to do."

The abruptness of his behavior added to Brianna's guilt. She reached out and touched Kevin's arm to keep him in the chair. "What did you to talk to me about?"

He looked at her hand. The stare made her feel like she was doing something wrong, and she pulled her hand into her lap, allowing him to stand.

"It's nothing." He walked to the door and put his hand on the knob. Brianna thought he was having the same trouble opening it as Doug had, but as he continued to stand there, she realized he wasn't trying to leave. She studied him and noticed his shoulders were shaking. Something was wrong.

Brianna walked to him and put her hand on his back. This time, he didn't shrug her off. He turned to her, and she gasped when she noticed the tears filling his eyes.

"Tell me," she said as she led him back to the chairs.

"Rosemary doesn't talk much about her mother," he said. "She steers clear of women in general. She connects best with male teachers, and she doesn't have a lot of friends."

Brianna didn't know what to say and nodded.

"But ever since she's been working puzzles with you, she's relaxed. I noticed it around the house. She talks about you, how you aren't interested in dating me—"

"She said that?" Brianna interrupted, then realized the implication of what she'd said. "I mean . . . you are dateable, but I'm off men. And, for the record, she's the one who told me you weren't dating again."

The grin on Kevin's face stopped her chatter. "I didn't take it personally. Sounds strange, but Rosemary and I have a good thing going, and now isn't the time to add someone else into the equation." His grin faded as he continued. "Her math teacher called me today, which is usually a bad sign. Mrs. Howard looks like Linda, and that upsets Rosemary. She acts out, and I get routine phone calls.

"But today's call was all about how Rosemary couldn't stop talking about her neighbor who's trying to solve a math problem for work."

Brianna nodded. "The receipts I can't get to add up."

"Exactly. Rosemary asked her teacher if she could help

solve the problem. Mrs. Howard called me to find out how to get in touch with you. She said anyone who can make Rosemary happy deserves to have someone help her in a tough situation."

Brianna sat there in disbelief. Someone she didn't know was offering to help her, all because she had been nice to Rosemary. This sort of thing didn't happen in real life. Only in books and movies. She started to tell Kevin this, but he stopped her.

"I don't know what happened to you, but whatever it was, it wasn't your fault. The person sitting in front of me is a kind person who respects others and goes out of her way to make sad twelve-year-olds happy. Something happened the night I brought Rosemary to your apartment, and I think that something is you. This is the first time since Linda died that my daughter has connected with another woman. She's making progress because of you."

Brianna wiped the stray tear that trickled down her face. "That's sweet. But I didn't do anything special with Rosemary. I treated her like I want people to treat me."

Kevin covered her hand with his and squeezed. The warmth of his palm reminded her how much she would miss her friends if she left. Her friends who wanted to help her avoid another mistake.

"You have people here who will help you figure this out. Talk to your boss. Don't run away. The only thing that will do is hurt the people who support you." He let go of her hand, stood up, and walked to the door. "The offer is still on the table. I'm good with numbers." He detoured back to where Philomena sat and picked up the plant. "I'm going to take this with me and see if Rosemary can nurse it back to health. She told me how attached you are to the plant. Maybe that will give you a reason to stay."

Brianna watched Kevin leave her apartment without saying goodbye. The door clicked shut behind him, and she lowered her head into her hands. Nothing of what Kevin had said should matter, but knowing that she'd changed Rosemary's life for the better made her feel good.

Maybe she did have people who cared for her and wanted to see her succeed. If she ran away, that would never happen. Still, she couldn't rely on Kevin to solve her problems. Relying on other people to fix her problems was what had gotten her to this position in the first place. But she could ask for help.

Which was exactly what she planned to do tomorrow morning. She would go to Raeburn and tell him everything, including the unbalanced receipts and statements and what Doug had shared tonight. Brianna grabbed the trash bags full of her stuff and headed to her bedroom.

She wasn't running away this time. This time, she would fight for what she wanted.

Chapter 35

The next morning, Brianna knocked on Kevin's apartment door. She shifted from one foot to the other. Kevin had been disappointed last night about her leaving. She hoped her news this morning would cheer him up.

Brianna's worry was cut short when Rosemary opened the door.

The girl frowned. "How come you killed Philomena?"

Brianna grimaced. "I didn't mean to. There's been a lot going on lately and I forgot to water her."

"That's not a good excuse. I'm twelve and even I know you have to water a plant," she said. She crossed her arms over her chest. "Dad gave her to me. I'm gonna resuscitate her like on that plant rescue show."

Having no idea what Rosemary was talking about, Brianna changed the subject. "I need to ask your dad for a favor. Could I talk to him?"

Rosemary looked over her shoulder. "He's in the shower."

Without waiting for a response, Rosemary turned back into the apartment.

Brianna followed Rosemary inside, where the girl sat at the

table to eat her breakfast, a bowl of oatmeal topped with blue-berries. Brianna nodded in approval.

"When I was your age, I ate sugary cereal. Nice job with the breakfast choice."

Rosemary shrugged and asked, "What's in the bag?"

"Remember those receipts we talked about? The ones that need a forensic accountant?"

She nodded as she chewed her food.

"Well, your dad offered to help me with them."

"He's no accountant," said Rosemary, a bite of oatmeal dribbling down her chin. She wiped it off with her sleeve. "How can he help?"

Brianna wondered the same thing, but she needed help, and Kevin and the math teacher had offered. She didn't think Rosemary needed all the details, though, and Brianna needed to get to work before Raeburn so she could fill him in on everything she'd learned from Doug.

"I'm going to head to work." She held out the tote bag. "Could you give this to your dad and ask him to give me a call?"

Rosemary stared at the bag but didn't take it. The silence made Brianna uncomfortable, and she was about to set the bag down when Rosemary said, "If you want to date my dad, it's okay with me."

Brianna's mouth opened, but nothing came out. Panick-ing, she closed it and started to speak again. This time, she was interrupted by Kevin's cough. Relief flowed through her as she met his gaze.

"Surprised you're here this morning. I wasn't sure if I'd see you again."

The relief turned to embarrassment and Brianna nodded. She ignored the way Rosemary's head went back and forth between her and Kevin and concentrated on the task at hand.

"I thought about what you said last night. This is the first time in my life I've had support like this, and I wasn't sure how to handle it. But if it's okay with you"—she held out the tote bag—"I'd like your help double-checking these. There's also a list of companies that might not be legitimate. The police are looking into them, too, but if you run across anything, let me know."

"If I can't do it, Mrs. Howard is around to help."

He took the bag from her. His fingers grazed her hand. Her skin buzzed at his touch, but she pulled back. It wasn't time for a relationship right now. She needed to get her situation back on track. Kevin caught her gaze and nodded.

Hoping he understood, Brianna turned to Rosemary. "Thank you for your permission to date your dad. But we're friends." Brianna grinned at Kevin. "And I'd like to keep it that way. Is that okay with you?"

Rosemary nodded, then put down her spoon. She hopped out of her seat and wrapped her arms around Brianna. Brianna returned the hug, all the while watching Kevin. Sometime soon, they needed to talk about what might happen to their relationship, but based on Rosemary's reaction, Brianna knew this was the best thing for the girl. And for her.

▭

CYNTHIA DROPPED her briefcase and started her computer. She'd left the house that morning without coffee. She couldn't bear to listen to her mother talk about the architectural plans for the pottery studio. While she waited for her computer to boot up, she headed to the break room.

She poured herself a cup of coffee and added a generous amount of cream and sugar. Cynthia knew it wouldn't work, but she hoped her extra-sweet coffee would take away some of the sting of not getting a new apartment. She'd followed Helene's advice and contacted Thomas, but it turned out she wasn't the only person using the relationship coordinator for real estate. The place had been snapped up before she talked to Thomas, but she extracted a promise from him: she got first dibs on the next one he heard about. Cynthia hoped it was before the demo crew arrived at her mother's house to start the pottery studio.

By the time she returned to her desk, the home screen on her computer stared back at her. She clicked her email app and began her morning routine of answering messages. Five responses into the process she frowned at the sight of Doug Gerome's name.

Cynthia stared at the screen. Doug was the last person she wanted to hear from. Nothing good ever came from him. He'd thrown a fit about the article she wrote when he had a car accident. The slime had gotten all charges dropped even though the entire town knew he was drunk when he'd crashed his rental car into a giant oak tree. Her piece had hinted that he'd paid someone off, but it wasn't the defamation that Doug claimed.

She leaned back in her chair and debated if she should open it. Knowing Doug, he had probably sent her a virus, too. But it looked like it would be a slow news day, and she needed something to keep her editor at bay. Helene's wedding column still ranked high, but it didn't hurt to have another hot story on the back burner.

Taking a deep breath, Cynthia clicked on Doug's message. She scanned it and did a double take when she digested the accusations Doug made.

"Holy guacamole."

Doug was back in full force. He had always liked to make trouble and point fingers at people, and he was doing exactly that. He called Carl Raeburn and his Women's Shelter and Support Agency into question. Doug accused Raeburn of leasing apartments to women who didn't deserve them as well as promising one level of accommodations and delivering another.

That weasel is taking advantage of struggling women, wrote Doug.

"Takes one to know one," Cynthia muttered as she took notes. As she reread the message, she shook her head. Several of the accusations didn't sound right. There were too many coincidences, including Doug's claim that Brianna Thompson was embezzling money and Sara Shaw knew about it. There was no mention of how he got this information or of Gwen Martin, the woman who'd been avoiding Cynthia's calls for weeks.

Her eye went back to the sentence about the weasel. She reread it several times before picking up her pen and underlining the phrase "struggling women." That didn't sound like Doug at all. Weasel wasn't his word of choice, either. "Asshat," "dipwad," or "son of a bitch" she would expect. But weasel? Not his brand of lingo.

In fact, the more she thought about it, the more certain she became. She'd known Doug for years and never once had he used the word *accommodations*. She doubted he knew what a promise was. The question was, If Doug didn't write this, who did?

The obvious choice was Brianna, who despised her ex. But Brianna seemed smarter than to implicate herself in a crime. Sara wouldn't be caught dead doing anything illegal, nor would her boss, Jared. And seeing as this was Raeburn's project, she didn't think he would want it to go badly either.

Which left Gwen. Cynthia's reporter brain churned through the possibilities. Why would Gwen bother to send a scoop like this? If it was true, Gwen could have gone to the authorities. If it was false, the story could be a smokescreen for something else going on.

Cynthia calculated how much time it would take her to vet the story. If a few phone calls confirmed it, then a major story like this would endear her to her editor for months. But if she could prove the information was false, there was still a story.

Why would someone want to spread lies about an organization set up to help those in need?

Grabbing her phone, Cynthia dialed Raeburn's number.

BRIANNA TWISTED her key in the office door. The stop at Kevin's house had taken longer than she'd planned, but she made it into work before Raeburn. Running away still sounded like a good idea, but seeing Kevin this morning had affirmed her decision. She would stay and fight for what was right: safe accommodations for women and children, and her reputation. And she didn't want to leave Rosemary behind.

As she opened the door, she heard the phone ringing. She rushed to her desk and grabbed it.

"Good morning. Raeburn Property Management. How can I help you?"

"This is Cynthia Anderson from *The Gazette*."

Brianna stifled a groan and settled down behind her desk.

"Is Mr. Raeburn in?"

Brianna turned on her computer. "He's not here. I expect him any minute. Is there anything I can help you with?"

"Is that you, Brianna?"

"Yes."

Cynthia paused. Brianna hoped the reporter would leave a message, but she winced when Cynthia said, "I never liked you much."

Rolling her eyes, Brianna shrugged. "I'm going to ignore that comment and leave a message for Mr. Raeburn."

She started to hang up when she heard Cynthia yell, "Wait! I know what's going on. Doug emailed me."

Brianna froze. Doug had been busy last night. With a sigh, she put the phone back to her ear. She refused to give Cynthia any details, but she needed to find out what the reporter suspected. "Okay. What did his email say?"

"He accused you of embezzling money."

The statement hung in the air before Brianna shook herself out of her silence. "Of course he did. Why wouldn't he? Even though he's the one removing furniture and appliances from apartments."

She heard paper shuffle on the other end of the line.

"Not according to him. He said you stole the stuff and gave the name of a couple of pawn shops and resale shops where you sold it. There's even a spreadsheet with original costs versus what the stuff sold for. He attached bank statements too. Supposedly, the deposits match up with the spreadsheet. And there are other deposits into the account. He said these will match the discrepancies on all the furniture orders for the last few months. Care to comment?"

Holding her head in her hands, Brianna processed what was happening. Doug had moved the furniture, but he didn't know anything about the discrepancies in the billings or the bank statement she could never reconcile. At least, she hadn't told him. Spreadsheets weren't his thing either. Nor was reaching out to anyone from his hometown. Doug knew people didn't like him and he didn't care.

Brianna's cell phone pinged, signaling an incoming text. She glanced down and saw it was from Kevin.

"Looked into the two companies you mentioned this morning. Both have been linked to a number of scams. I'll email the details."

"I assume your silence means I can run the story."

Cynthia's voice broke Brianna's concentration. She still didn't understand what was going on, but she suspected Doug wasn't behind it. "I wouldn't if I were you."

"Oh? And why not?"

"Doug isn't our bad guy. There's a story here, but I think we need to put our heads together and figure this out."

Chapter 36

Brianna and Cynthia compared notes the entire morning. They discovered that the email address used to send Cynthia the documents was an alias of Gwen's work email. Since both knew Doug wasn't tech-savvy enough to figure out how to do that, the evidence pointed at one person: Gwen Martin.

A call from Kevin sealed the deal.

"I'm sending you a spreadsheet," he'd explained when she put him on speakerphone so Cynthia could hear. "Mrs. Howard and I worked on this separately, but we both got the same result. All the discrepancies in the bills were credited to the same account. We've got the last four digits. That isn't much, but it will get you started. Did you get my text about the companies?"

Brianna stared at the digits, and a smile spread across her face. The digits matched the bank account number she could never get to reconcile.

"Thank you! This helps a ton. And so did the text."

She imagined the smile on Kevin's face was as wide as hers.

"That's great news. You'll have to tell me how you got it

later. I've got to get to work. Rosemary and I will stop by tonight to celebrate."

Brianna made a mental note to stop at the store for some decent food to entertain her guests. Now that she knew who was behind the theft in the office, she was reasonably sure she would have a job for the near future. She could afford to splurge on something better than ramen.

"But why would she do this?" asked Cynthia. "Raeburn had nothing but good things to say about her. She's been an employee for years. I mean, she refused to return my phone calls, but that doesn't mean she's behind this."

"She's not pleasant to work with," Brianna said. "Maybe she has a compulsive shopping problem. Those designer shoes aren't cheap. Trust me."

Brianna thought she heard a hint of irritation in Cynthia's voice. "Just because I live in a small town doesn't mean I don't know my designers. We've got internet."

"Fair enough." Brianna laughed, realizing the presumption she'd made. "I need to get all this stuff to Mr. Raeburn and the police department."

Cynthia's protest caught her off guard. "What about my breaking story? I can't use this information if it's an ongoing investigation."

As much as Brianna appreciated Cynthia's help, the reporter was right. It would be several days before the police would release the results of the case, and by then, someone else with less ethical convictions could scoop Cynthia. She thought about the options and made the only suggestion she could.

"What if I can get Mr. Raeburn to give you another exclusive interview once this is over? Would that make dealing with your editor easier?"

Cynthia's enthusiasm caught Brianna off guard. "Absolutely! Keep the reporters away from him. For as long as you can."

Once that was set, the women said goodbye and Brianna relaxed back in her chair. It felt good to be on this side of a bad situation for once. Solving a problem felt better than causing one.

All that was left now was to get Raeburn up to speed and figure out where Gwen was. Brianna checked the clock and was surprised to see it was almost lunchtime. Raeburn should have been here by now. Brianna checked her email and text messages, but none of them gave her any clues.

Something didn't seem right about the situation. Raeburn always showed up on time. She thought back to her conversation with him the night before. It seemed like ages ago after all the other things she'd been through, but she distinctly remembered him saying they would discuss things in the morning. *This* morning.

Before she let herself get too worried, she pulled the detective's business card from her pocket and dialed his number. The call went to voicemail, and she left a message.

"Hello, this is Brianna Thompson. I spoke with you yesterday with Carl Raeburn about some missing items from his rental units. I received some information I think is important to the case. And I was wondering if you've talked to Mr. Raeburn. He planned to come in this morning, but he never showed up at the office."

She left her callback number, then hung up the phone.

Brianna looked around. She wasn't sure what else she could do but wait. Sitting still wasn't something she enjoyed. She hopped up and went to Gwen's office to see what she could find.

As soon as she opened the door, she knew something was off. The Eiffel Tower pictures were missing, and the usual floral scent had grown stale. Instead of sneezing, Brianna's nose tickled. She ignored it as she stepped to the desk and noticed several of the drawers sticking out. Curiosity set in as she thumbed through the files.

She couldn't tell for sure, but some of the files seemed to be missing. Brianna pushed in the drawer and noticed a small piece of paper on the floor. She bent down to pick it up and drew in a sharp breath. It was the business card the detective had given Raeburn the day before. For some reason, her boss had been in Gwen's office. Which meant he'd been here this morning.

"Where are you now?" she asked out loud as she turned the card over in her hand. The address of the apartment they'd visited the day before, *"6 E. Main, Apt 2B,"* was scribbled in Raeburn's handwriting. Whatever was going on, she needed to get to the bottom of it. Racing back to her desk, she dialed Shelby's phone number. Her friend picked up on the first ring.

"Did you change your mind?" Shelby asked brightly.

Brianna paused. So much had changed. She didn't know where to start, but she knew Shelby was referring to her plan to leave town.

"Yes. But that's not why I'm calling. I need your help. More specifically, your car. Any way you can pick me up right now at my office? I need to check on something at one of the apartments."

"I'm glad you're staying, but I'm walking into work right now. Sorry." Brianna heard the casino noises chiming in the background. "But why don't you call Kevin? He owes you one, doesn't he?"

Grabbing her purse, Brianna said, "I already collected this morning." She regretted her words when she heard Shelby chuckle.

"Hmm. Sounds interesting. Do tell."

"Get your mind out of the gutter. He helped me with some financial reports."

"Blah. I like my idea better." Brianna heard someone call out Shelby's name. "I gotta go. Floor manager broke up with his girlfriend. I'm picking up her shifts. Sorry I can't help."

Glad for her friend, Brianna focused on her situation. She couldn't call Kevin. She didn't want to call a taxi or ride share. The bus didn't interest her either. She needed to get to the apartment fast, though. She scrolled through her contact list to check her options. She shook her head when she thought of one person who might be willing to help. With a sigh, she dialed the number.

Chapter 37

"Alex, thanks for coming over on such short notice," said Brianna as she double-checked her seat belt. She'd never ridden with Alex before, but his driving shouldn't have surprised her. He was a maniac on and off the road. "I wasn't sure what you would say when I called."

Her former boss glanced over at her as he whipped his red Maserati around a minivan. Brianna slid in the leather seat, and she grabbed the door handle to steady herself.

"What the hell! Don't open the door!" Alex cried. "You fling that open and someone will hit it. And you can't afford to pay for a new door—even with your fancy new salary!"

Brianna wished for the tenth time that she'd splurged for a ride share, but Alex was faster and cheaper. Plus, he was concerned about Raeburn as well.

"How could I turn you down? I'm worried about Carl. That man never misses a meeting, and he missed two this morning. If you think he's at the apartment, I want to be there in case something is wrong."

Another left-hand turn and the car screeched to a halt in front of the apartment building. Relief rushed through Brianna, but she didn't dwell on it. She jabbed at the release button on the seat belt. As soon as she was free, she dashed up the walk and flung open the lobby door. Running up the steps, she was barely breathing hard when she reached 2B. She started to put the key in the lock but noticed the door was ajar.

Fear came over her. Gwen didn't seem like a violent person, but what if she was working with someone who was? It dawned on Brianna that she should have called the police before she left the office. Her courage wavered, and she was still standing there when Alex came up.

Wheezing as if it had been ten flights instead of two, he bent over and put his hands on his knees.

"Power drinkin' . . . " Alex paused to take three deep breaths before he continued, "ain't good exercise after all."

Brianna shook her head. "Alex, we need backup. You're a mess, and this door isn't locked. What if Gwen is waiting in there with a two-by-four?"

"No way she could balance in her stilettos holding a piece of lumber."

"Should I call the police?" Brianna couldn't argue with Alex's logic, but she didn't want to get in over her head.

"And tell them what? Your boss isn't in the office, and you think he's been kidnapped. Brianna, the man hasn't been missing long enough for anyone to care."

"Then why are you here helping me?"

"Because we both know something isn't right." He stood upright and took a couple more deep breaths. "Okay. I'm good. You wanna get behind me in case someone attacks?"

The possibility that Alex would protect her made her want to laugh, but she didn't want to offend him. He'd already done more than she expected of him.

Brianna nodded to the door. "I'll be fine. Let's go."

She pushed the door open slowly. The lights were on in the living room. She glanced around the room and noticed that the original furniture was back in its place. She moved into the kitchen, keeping her eyes open for anyone or anything that shouldn't be there. Opening a few drawers, she found all the glasses, flatware, and plates she had ordered were back in place.

She turned around and jumped when she saw Alex standing right behind her. "What are you doing?"

He shrugged. "You went first. I'm following. I really don't want to get hit. I can tell you from experience it isn't fun."

While she knew he was trying to lighten the mood, Brianna was on edge. Things were exactly the way they should have been when Sara and Jared came to visit. Why would someone change them now?

The hair on Brianna's neck raised when she heard a groan from somewhere in the apartment. "Did you hear that?" she whispered to Alex, who was pulling out his cell phone.

"I did, and I'm calling the police now. This is too much for us. For me." He headed back to the front door. "I'll be outside to show them the way up. Don't get hurt."

Before she could call out to him, Alex disappeared. She heard the noise again, and Brianna knew she had no choice but to investigate. She opened the drawer and pulled out the wooden rolling pin she'd placed in all the apartments. She imagined it being used for pie crusts, but self-defense worked too.

The first room she checked was empty, as was the second. By the time she got to the third, nervousness consumed her. The rolling pin shook as she raised her arm. She took a deep breath and opened the last bedroom door.

Lying on the bed staring at her was Raeburn, his mouth covered with a strip of duct tape and his hands and feet bound.

Remembering all the scary movies she'd ever watched, Brianna froze in place. Someone might be lurking in the corner or under the bed or in the attached bathroom. She put her finger to her lips to indicate to Raeburn to be quiet, but he shook his head. Cautiously, she searched the room, but there was no one there.

She approached the bed slowly, in case someone was hiding under it, but when she saw no one was there, she raced the rest of the way and ripped off the tape.

"Damn, that hurt!" Raeburn lifted his arms. "Could you get me out of this? It's cutting off my circulation."

"Are you okay? I mean, other than being tied up?"

He nodded. "Yes, and I'd be happy to explain what happened as soon as I can feel my fingers and toes again."

Brianna ran to the kitchen and pulled a pair of scissors from the drawer. She started back to the bedroom and had him unbound in less than a minute. While he rubbed his wrists and ankles, she texted Alex.

Mr. Raeburn's fine. ETA on police?

"Who are you texting?" asked Raeburn.

"Alex drove me over. He's calling the police."

Raeburn gaped. "Nice to know he cared enough to help find me."

Her phone pinged, and she read Alex's response.

OTW.

While they waited, Brianna helped Raeburn hobble to the living room. She settled him on the couch before heading to the kitchen to get him a glass of water and return the rolling pin to its rightful spot.

"I can't believe she'd do something like this," he said after he'd taken a sip. "I trusted her. After all the years I've spent training her, this is how she thanks me."

They turned toward the front door where they heard footsteps. Alex's head peeked into the apartment.

"Everyone okay? No blood anywhere, right? I can't stand blood."

Rolling her eyes, Brianna nodded. "The coast is clear." As soon as Alex entered the apartment, Brianna turned to Raeburn. "What happened?"

"My wife and I talked last night about everything we found yesterday. I mentioned the shoe thing to her, and she agreed. Unless those were all . . . ," he paused, struggling to find the word, "knockoffs . . . yeah, that's what my wife called it . . . then Gwen couldn't have paid for them on her salary. Maybe she had some money saved up, but my wife said with the number of shoes I described, it made sense that Gwen needed money."

"How did you get here?" she asked.

"Yes, well. I went to the office this morning. I'd left my files for my meetings with Alex on my desk. When I got there, I heard Gwen in her office." He stopped and frowned. "She was stuffing files into a briefcase when I knocked on the door. She told me she was leaving and couldn't work with you anymore. I asked her why and then everything went black. When I woke up, I was here. How did you find me?"

She handed him the business card she found in Gwen's office, and he nodded.

"I planned to call the detective after my appointments with Alex."

"No need to call me now," the detective said as he pushed open the door. He shook his head. "I'd say it's nice to see you, but something tells me this situation is even more confusing than before."

A paramedic stuck his head into the apartment. "We got a call about a kidnapping victim."

The detective waved him in. Soon, the living room was full of paramedics, firefighters, and police officers.

"This is overkill, don't you think?" asked Alex as the emergency workers strapped Raeburn to a gurney.

Brianna shook her head. "They need to make sure he's okay. Plus, the detective is looking for evidence against Gwen."

"Her fingerprints will be here anyway. She helped set up the apartment."

Brianna knew he was right, but with the apartment in its

original condition, there was nothing for them to find here. Which meant Gwen and Doug got away scot-free—again, in Doug's case. She didn't know how he managed it, but her ex-boyfriend never suffered any consequences.

"Come on. I'll drive you back to the office," Alex said, interrupting her thoughts. "You've got to keep it running while Carl's out of commission."

Raeburn called out his agreement. "Yes, Brianna. Please! I shouldn't be out long. Call Jared and Sara if you need anything. They can help."

Pleased that he trusted her but nervous about working with Sara, Brianna knew she was up for the challenge. But there was no way she was riding with Alex again.

Whipping out her cell phone, she called up her ride share app and booked a car.

"Alex, you're off the hook. There's a car coming right this way that can take me back." She ignored the sad look on his face and waved to Raeburn. "Don't worry about a thing. The office will be ready when you get back."

Chapter 38

When Brianna's ride share pulled up in front of Raeburn's office, her eyebrows raised at the sight of all the activity. Several police cars sat in the parking lot. An officer stood next to the front door while several others milled around outside. She noticed Alex's red Maserati parked on the street and smiled. It would be nice to have a familiar face in all the chaos.

As the ride share drove off, Alex jogged toward her. "What took you so long?"

"We drove the speed limit, thank you." She gestured at the office. "Have you talked to anyone?"

"The detective sent over a list of people allowed inside. It's you and me, Jared and Sara. You sure you can handle this?" He looked at his watch. "I've got some time before my next appointment. I can stay if you want."

Brianna smiled. She liked seeing this side of Alex. "I'm okay." She motioned to the police. "If Gwen or Doug are there, which they won't be, the authorities can handle it. I can't say for sure about Gwen, but Doug is long gone by now."

Alex's head bounced like a bobblehead doll. He kept nodding until she stepped closer to the building.

"Thanks for your help today. I couldn't have done it without you."

"Yes, you could have. You're stronger than you give your-self credit for."

She stared at Alex, wondering if she'd heard him correctly.

"What?" He shrugged. "I should have told you sooner, but I'm telling you now. Stop letting people take advantage of you. You're more than capable."

As she watched him walk to his car, Brianna re-evaluated her opinion of Alex. She didn't want to work for him again, but she saw what a good friend he was to Raeburn. She hadn't given Alex enough credit.

"His driving still sucks," she said as she watched the red car fly down the street accompanied by horns blaring. Brianna watched until he screeched around the corner before she turned to the office.

A police officer greeted her at the door. After confirming her identify, he said, "All clear. As far as we can tell, everything looks fine. Our instructions are to wait here for the rest of the day, but it's safe for you to go inside."

Brianna thanked the officer and got right to work. She assembled a history of all billing discrepancies. Between everything Cynthia, Kevin and Mrs. Howard had confirmed, she now had a complete picture of the damage. She researched how much money the two fake vendors had been paid. It turned out Gwen had paid them, or rather herself, thousands of dollars over the years.

Doubtful they'd ever find the money, Brianna moved on to the next order of business: calling Sara. Raeburn might think Sara and Jared supported her, but she wasn't sure. She needed to know firsthand how Sara would react. Plus, she wanted permission to get Lorraine out of the apartment and Suzanne in it.

Before she could look up Sara's number, the phone rang.

"Raeburn Property Management," Brianna said as she grabbed her notebook. "How can I help you?"

"Brianna, it's Sara. Jared just got off the phone with Mr. Raeburn's wife. She told him what happened. Are you okay? And why are you at the office? Is it safe there?"

It took a second to figure out which question to answer first, but Brianna assumed the attorney would be most concerned with the office.

"The police searched the office. It's fine."

"What about you?" Sara asked again. "You've had a rough day."

"That's the understatement of the year." Brianna sighed. She might as well tell Sara what she wanted to know. "I'm fine. Mr. Raeburn said I could give you a call if anything came up. I was actually looking up your number when you called."

"What can I help you with?"

"I want to fix something else Gwen ruined, and I need your advice on how to do it without causing Mr. Raeburn any more problems than necessary."

Brianna explained the situation with Lorraine and Suzanne and asked what the best way was to get the apartment to its rightful renter.

"Give Suzanne a call and offer her the apartment, and I'll take care of Lorraine."

"Just like that?" This was another thing that felt too easy. "I thought there would be a bunch of paperwork or convincing for you to do."

"No. I can fix this in my sleep. Whatever we can do to make sure the agency does the maximum amount of benefit, I'm on board. Call Suzanne."

Rather than question the offer, Brianna did as she was

told. She was a bit giddy as she looked up Suzanne's phone number and made the call.

"Hello?"

Brianna heard boys' voices in the background.

"Hi, this is Brianna Thompson at the Women's Shelter and Support Agency. Can I speak with Suzanne, please?"

"This is Suzanne. Who are you again?"

"I work for the agency that provides reduced-cost housing. You interviewed with us a few weeks ago."

The noise in the background got louder, and the woman said, "Can you hold on? I need to take care of something." Brianna couldn't make out exactly what was happening, but it sounded like she was refereeing a boxing match. A minute later, Suzanne came back on the line, sounding a bit winded. "Okay. I remember you. You're the one who said my sons were too wild and crazy to be allowed into a brand-new apartment. You said I would have better luck finding someplace to live at the zoo."

Shocked by her frankness, Brianna blurted out, "I didn't say that. I would never say anything like that, but I'm not surprised Gwen did."

"Whoever it was didn't mince words. She said not to bother applying again, which I don't intend to do. If I want to be insulted, I'll talk to my ex-husband. So, if you don't mind, I need to attend to the children before someone calls animal control."

"Wait!" Brianna cried. She didn't expect to get this much pushback from Suzanne. She'd assumed the woman would be happy to hear from her. But Brianna didn't know if she could keep her attention long enough to explain. "There was a mistake. You get an apartment."

The line fell silent, and for a minute, Brianna thought Suzanne had hung up on her.

But then Suzanne asked, "Are you serious?"

"Yes. You should have gotten it the first time around.

There was a misunderstanding of sorts." Brianna looked down at her desk and took a deep breath. "It's yours if you want it."

"For real? This isn't a practical joke?"

"It may take a week or two to get things cleared out and set up, but I assure you this is not a joke. I've seen your file, and this is the least we can do to help you get back on your feet."

Chapter 39

"So, you think we've seen the last of Gwen?"

The expression on Raeburn's face made Brianna's heart ache. She knew what it was like when someone you trusted let you down. She could only imagine how he felt knowing that the person he put in charge of his office for the last few years wasn't who he thought she was.

Maybe it was easier for Brianna to accept because she hadn't known Gwen that long and because she'd been through this with Doug before. Not everyone was honest.

"According to what the police found, yes, I think we have."

Gwen's trail had gone cold after her phone and ID were found a few weeks after Raeburn was kidnapped. They suspected she was using false identification, but until they had more leads they couldn't do anything more.

"Are you ready to be in charge of all this?"

Brianna nodded. "I am. Thank you for believing in me despite all that's happened."

Raeburn shrugged. "It's water under the bridge. Tell me, how are Suzanne's kids doing in the new place? Do they like it?"

"Suzanne thinks so. Having someplace to call their own

instead of the women's shelter made a big change in her boys' behavior." She took a deep breath. Brianna wanted to make sure Raeburn knew how much she appreciated him trusting her, even when she hadn't been completely honest about her past with Doug and Sara. "And thank you again for keeping me on. I can't tell you how much I appreciate it."

Waving away her comment, Raeburn smiled. "You've been great. Who else would have thought to come look for me at the apartment?"

Brianna frowned at the thought of what would have happened if they hadn't found him. He was healthy enough, but no one did well when they were gagged and bound. Gwen had tied him up and left him in the apartment to give herself enough time to get away.

A side benefit of Gwen's fall from grace was that Brianna and Sara were getting along. Sara contacted her daily to keep apprised of the business. They'd even shared a joke earlier that week. It wasn't much, but it was proof that Brianna was moving in the right direction.

Raeburn checked his watch. "We need to get moving for our two o'clock appointment."

Brianna pulled up her calendar. "I don't have anything on my schedule until four. What do you need me to bring?" Since Gwen had left, it wasn't unusual for Brianna to help Raeburn with his meetings, although he usually gave her plenty of notice.

He stood up and patted his pockets. "Yourself. I have everything else covered. We can walk to the place."

Confused by her involvement in a meeting she knew nothing about, Brianna grabbed her purse and followed him out of the office. Brianna walked down the sidewalk beside him, content to make their journey in silence. She'd learned that her boss would tell her what she needed to know when she needed to know it, unlike Gwen, who didn't tell her anything. At least not until it was too late.

They'd only walked a few minutes when Raeburn turned down a side street Brianna hadn't explored yet.

"Where are we going?" she asked.

He pointed to a single-story white building. "There. I told Jared and Sara we'd meet them."

Brianna crinkled her forehead. This didn't look like the typical purchase for the Women's Shelter and Support Agency, but maybe he was trying something new.

Sort of like her life.

It was a different feeling now that she had a lot to be happy about. Her job allowed her to help people. Her own apartment had finally fallen into place with the help of her insurance check. And Kevin and Rosemary had accepted her invitation to dinner to thank them for all their help. Things were looking up.

Then, she physically looked up and realized where Raeburn was taking her.

The sign for the Wedding Chapel hung lopsided, with one of the screws coming loose from the corner. The neon light in the *C* flickered. To the casual observer, it could have been *hapel* instead of *Chapel*.

Their destination startled her, and she halted on the sidewalk in front of the double doors.

"Who's getting married?"

Raeburn tugged open the door and motioned for Brianna to enter ahead of him. "I told you. We're meeting Jared and Sara. They need us to help with something."

It dawned on her what was going on, but her eyes still got wide when she saw Elvis standing by the guest book next to the chapel door.

"Aren't you a sight for sore eyes?" he said as he held out the pen. "Jot your name down here and we'll get this ceremony *all shook up!*"

He dropped the pen into Brianna's open hand as she turned back to Raeburn.

"You know, I thought things were getting back to normal. Now I'm not sure. Elvis at a wedding chapel isn't usually on my afternoon agenda."

He smiled back at her as he took the pen from her hand and signed the book. "But you're enjoying it, aren't you?" He took Brianna's hand and wrapped her fingers around the pen.

"I'll have to see what kind of cake they serve!" she giggled.

Her boss laughed and waited while she scrawled her name next to his. She looked up when Elvis called out, "Gotta warm up for *Blue Moon*. It's everybody's favorite," and ran off down the dimmed hallway.

"Allow me." Raeburn held a corsage in his hand. It matched the boutonniere that had mysteriously appeared on his lapel. She stood there as he pinned the flowers to her shirt and promptly sneezed when the scent of lilies hit her nose.

"Sorry about that." She sneezed again. "Allergic to lilies."

Raeburn shook his head and unpinned the flowers. He tossed them on the hall table and guided Brianna toward the doors to the chapel.

"I'm sure Sara will be okay without the flowers. Although you should take a few steps away from her, because I'm guessing her bouquet has lilies." Offering his arm, he asked, "Shall we?"

Brianna took her boss's arm and let him lead her into the chapel. She lost the power of speech at the sight that greeted her.

Sara and Jared stood at the front of the chapel by the altar. Sara looked back at her in a white halter dress that could have come straight from the courtroom but still looked feminine enough for a wedding. Her brunette hair nestled at the base of her neck in a smooth bun, and teardrop earrings sparkled from her earlobes.

Jared took Sara's hand, and Brianna couldn't help smiling. Jared's simple summer suit fit him like a glove, and the pale gray complemented the bride's dress.

"Bet you didn't see this one coming," Sara said to Brianna.

Shaking her head, Brianna said, "Actually, it makes sense. The two of you together, that is. But what am *I* doing here?"

Raeburn squeezed her arm. "They need witnesses. I volunteered us. I hope that's okay."

Brianna stood up a little straighter. Being a witness for a wedding was an important task. She nodded but paused. "What about your sister? Or your mother? Didn't they want to be here?"

"Actually, this was Mom's idea. She's been writing a column in the newspaper, and one of the articles is about eloping." Sara gestured around the chapel. "Plus, Tasha's hosting a big party for us next time we're in Glen Valley. In case you're wondering, it was Tasha who suggested we ask you to be a witness for us."

Jared nodded in agreement. "She wanted someone who knows the family to be here with us today. We could have paid Elvis the extra twenty bucks—"

"Don't forget the twenty we would have to pay Marilyn Monroe. We have to have two witnesses." Sara kissed Jared on the cheek after she interrupted him.

Happiness reflected off Jared, and he nodded. "Fine. Forty dollars. Anyway, Tasha wanted us to find someone with a little history. Carl has been my business partner for years. Sara's known of you for almost as long, although in the last few weeks she's gotten to know you better."

Sara walked to where Brianna was standing and squeezed her shoulder. "You've done so much. If it weren't for you, Mr. Raeburn's project wouldn't still be running. You stepped in when you were needed. Even when Gwen said those horrible things about you, you didn't crack. That means I was wrong. I'm sorry I disrespected you, and I'd like to be friends. Starting now. Will you please be a witness at my wedding?"

Of all the things that had happened in her life, this wedding felt like the strangest. Most people didn't get called to be a witness at a wedding with Elvis in their lifetimes, nor for someone who couldn't stand them only a few months prior.

Even though Brianna felt uncomfortable with the situation, Sara's offer was genuine. For once, she felt like she was part of something greater than herself. It was like she had a new family.

"Sure, I'll be your witness." She winked at the bride. "But only if I get a dance with Elvis."

Sara laughed. She leaned in as if she were going to give Brianna a hug but stopped. Brianna frowned before she realized this was Sara's way of telling her she could decide. Did she want to be friends with Sara after all the drama of the past? Brianna knew Tasha had accepted her apology, but she didn't know she needed Sara's forgiveness, too, until it was right in front of her.

Being careful not to wrinkle Sara's beautiful wedding dress, Brianna enveloped the bride in a hug.

"Thank you," she whispered. "I didn't know I needed this."

Just then, Elvis's booming voice came over the speakers. "Time to get this wedding moving. It's time for *Today, Tomorrow, and Forever.*"

Chapter 40

Brianna jogged up the stairs to her apartment. She balanced the bag of groceries on her hip while she unlocked the door with her free hand. It took Sara's help to understand her lease, but her landlord had finally fixed the lock.

She dropped her purse on her new end table and took her groceries to the kitchen. Ever since Brianna had witnessed the wedding the previous month, Sara had treated her differently.

Thinking about the wedding made her smile. Brianna made a mental note that if she ever did get married, she would go to the Wedding Chapel. The officiant was nice, and Elvis's songs were fabulous. She hadn't heard a version of *Teddy Bear* that rivaled the 1957 version, but this rendition came close. This Elvis was the one she wanted.

She glanced around the room at the furniture she'd purchased to replace the stuff Naomi had stolen, and it looked good.

"Better than good. Freaking awesome!" she said as she congratulated herself on making good choices. The bright-blue couch rested on the edge of a fluffy white carpet. Throw pillows in white and yellow dotted the couch and comple-mented the two swivel side chairs she'd chosen to round out the living space. A silver milk pail sat at attention in the middle of the reclaimed wood coffee table.

She swept her fingers over the back of the couch. A lightweight afghan would be a nice addition. Brianna made a mental note to look for one on Suzanne's new online shop. Since she'd gotten settled and the kids were in school, Suzanne spent what free time she had making crafts and blankets to sell. She had a way to go, but the woman was getting back on her feet. Smiling at Suzanne's improvement, Brianna made her way back to her bedroom.

She couldn't believe her luck as she glanced at the gray upholstered headboard she'd added on impulse. She didn't need it, but it had been on clearance and the salesperson gave her an extra discount when she mentioned she was working at the Women's Shelter and Support Agency.

"Anyone who stands up for women deserves all the help they can get."

Brianna sprawled on the gray-and-white-patterned comforter and shook her head in disbelief. Not only did she have a furnished apartment again, but she also had a job that meant something to her. And she'd prevented Doug from ruining yet another thing in her life.

The doorbell rang, and she jumped off the bed. Kevin had promised to bring Rosemary over. His daughter had some ideas for wall hangings. Brianna had spent most of her budget on furniture, but Rosemary suggested they glue together some of the puzzles they'd worked to use as decorations.

Not bothering to look out the peephole, Brianna pulled the door open and was surprised to see Kevin standing by himself, a bouquet of sunflowers in his hands.

"Hi!" he said as he handed her the flowers. "Rosemary picked these out. She knows you like sunflowers."

Brianna took the bouquet and motioned for Kevin to come in. She peeked into the hallway when he entered her apartment. "Where's Rosemary? She promised to help me decorate."

"She told me to apologize for her and she'll come by later this weekend." He paused, and a huge grin covered his face. "She got invited to a friend's house to hang out."

Brianna halted on her way to the kitchen. Her mouth dropped open in disbelief. "That's amazing news. I'm happy for her." She took in Kevin's relaxed posture and the glow on his face. "And for you. How does it feel not to have her next to you?"

"Different, that's for sure. Her friend picked her up about an hour ago. I sat in the apartment and stared at the wall." He shook his head. "Not sure what to do. I didn't think we'd get to this point. She hasn't wanted to fit in since Linda died, and now she's making progress. Which wouldn't have happened without you."

He touched her arm, and Brianna smiled. It was great that Rosemary seemed to be growing up, despite the pain she'd endured with her mother's death. And nice to know she could have a male friend without complications.

"Come on," she said as she picked up the milk pail from the table. "I'll put the sunflowers in water. Do you want something to drink?"

"No, I'm fine."

She took the flowers and the container to the kitchen. As she added water, she sensed Kevin standing behind her. Looking over her shoulder, she frowned. The expression on his face worried her. The smile was still there, but his eyes held sadness.

"Are you okay?"

As she looked at him, she noticed his shoulders rise as if he were taking a deep breath. Kevin blew it out and nodded.

"Better than I ever thought I would be." He paused and looked around the kitchen. "Are you going to get a new roommate?"

Brianna turned off the faucet and shrugged. "I'm not sure I'm ready to live with someone else, especially after what Naomi did. But money's a little tight. I might not have a choice." She hesitated, then continued, "Mr. Raeburn offered to let me rent one of the agency's apartments, but I hate to take up space when another family needs it more than me."

"Without a doubt I can tell you Rosemary wants you to stay. She loves having you close by and has a new puzzle waiting for you." He followed her and sat down on the couch. "It's selfish, but I hope you stay too. I like hanging out with you."

Brianna placed the flowers on the table, arranging them to stall for time. She liked Kevin, but both knew they weren't ready for a relationship. She had finally figured out how to be strong on her own, without relying on a man to make her whole. It would be risky to start a relationship now. Things might end like they had with her past relationships.

She jumped when she felt Kevin's hand cover hers.

"You're overthinking this thing. Don't get caught up in it. I'm not in any hurry. Maybe we work out, but if we don't, that's fine with me. I'm happy to have you as a friend."

She dabbed at her eyes as they filled with tears. "It's not that I don't like you. I like *me* more now that I know what I'm capable of. But I haven't had enough time to be on my own to see what I can accomplish. I've never trusted myself enough to believe I can do it on my own. It really isn't you. This is all about me."

Kevin squeezed her hand and nodded. "You've come a long way. Don't forget that." He stood up and let himself out the door.

As it closed behind him, Brianna felt a combination of sadness and strength. She liked Kevin, and she had a feeling they would make a good couple. And Rosemary was the best. Brianna wished she could give them what they needed. But if the last month had taught her anything, it was that she didn't need to base her self-worth on anyone other than herself.

For the first time in her entire life, Brianna knew that she could do this on her own. She didn't need to gamble to make things pay off.

About the Author

Carole Wolfe writes women's fiction that makes you smile. She enjoys running at a leisurely pace, crocheting baby blankets for others and drinking wine when she can find the time. After moving nine times in twenty years, Carole and her family have settled in Texas.

Follow Carole at www.carolewolfe.com.

Also by Carole Wolfe

My Best Series

My Best Mistake - Tasha's Story

My Best Decision - Sara's Story

My Best Memory - Helene's Story

My Best Gamble - Brianna's Story

www.ingramcontent.com/pod-product-compliance
Lightning Source LLC
Chambersburg PA
CBHW072009210726

48294CB00013B/1744